# DEATH IN THE HEADLIGHTS

## A KYLE CALLAHAN MYSTERY FEATURING DETECTIVE LINDA

Mark McNease

ISBN: 0615981097
ISBN 13: 9780615981093

MadeMark Publishing
New York City
www.mademarkpublishing.com

*And be sure to visit the Kyle Callahan Mysteries website:*
www.kcallahanmysteries.com

For Ken Davis-Hlenczuk and Rick Rose

"It's friendship, friendship,
just a perfect blend ship …" – Cole Porter

*Time is the most valuable gift we give one another.*

*Thank you for the decades
and the laughter.*

"Whatever grows there, grows in the shadows."

– Clara Presley's grandmother

# CHAPTER ONE

Abigail Creek sat on her bed about to watch a horror movie. Halloween was two weeks away but already the stations were playing reruns of *The Exorcist* and *Friday the 13th*, versions one through twelve. She'd only seen the first one. She didn't care much for sequels, and was delighted that John Carpenter's original *Halloween,* 1978, with young scream queen Jamie Lee Curtis, was showing tonight. It was almost enough to make her glad she was too sick to go to dinner with the family. Correction, the family *and Charlotte.* The five of them were behaving as a unit more often since the divorce negotiations had reached their final phase. Abigail hated the act she'd put on throughout the process, pretending it was all fine with her: sixty-two years old and being usurped by a woman twenty years younger who was once her dearest friend, a woman she had introduced to her husband Clarence. A woman who had all but moved into CrossCreek Farm, befriending the family, preparing to become the new matriarch as Abigail graciously and quietly stepped aside. *Oh, have I got a surprise for you,* she thought, settling in against the headboard with a bowl of freshly popped corn and a tall glass of Alka-Seltzer. She had no idea if it was the right thing to take for the stomach cramps that struck her late in the day, an unforeseen and sudden illness she attributed to the stress she was under. She was feeling noticeably better now and thought she might be on the mend enough to enjoy the movie without doubling over in pain. Whatever it was, it was passing; too late for dinner with the others, but maybe that was why she had taken ill in the first place, a psychosomatic solution to a problem not easily solved.

John Carpenter's simple, eerie score began as the movie started. Abigail couldn't believe it had been thirty-six years since she first saw the movie on its release, watching through her fingers at the scariest parts. Her heart felt a stab at the memory: she had been with Clarence then, in her mid-twenties and madly in love. She had gripped his hand throughout the movie, and had believed, then and up until just this past year, that she would be holding his hand until they day she died.

*Let it go, Abi*, she told herself. *He has betrayed you, let it go. Set the trap, pull the spring, be patient.*

She had just taken her first handful of popcorn from the bowl when she heard it. A creaking sound. A footstep. *A footstep?* That's silly, she told herself, even as she felt the hair rise on her arms. It's just a creak. *Why do you think they call it CrossCreek Farm*, she asked herself, smiling. Cross*Creak*. Of course it creaks. It's old and large and … empty. Empty except for Abigail—and the alarm. Clarence always turned it on when he left. He kept it on when they were at home, too, unlike many homeowners who don't realize the most valuable thing they can protect is themselves. The only sound there should be reason to jump at was the alarm going off.

She took another handful of popcorn and tried to focus on the movie. Jamie Lee was so young then. And now she made yogurt commercials, looking mature but still radiant. Abigail wondered if it was the yogurt that preserved her so well.

The sound of a creak came again. It wasn't the sound of the house settling or floorboards adjusting to the cooler temperatures. It was the sound of someone in the house. Had one of them come home for some reason? Maybe her stomach problem was catching. But that made no sense; they'd driven in one car. Had they all returned?

"Clarence?" she called out. "Caroline? Are you back already?"

There was no reply, and the creaking stopped.

She reached for the remote and muted the television. She listened carefully in the silence. She knew better than to call out again. It was too late not to let an intruder know she'd heard him. Or had she simply heard the house moaning and settling? Then the creak came again and she knew she was not alone. She slipped out of bed, looking quickly around for her cell phone. Where had she left it? In the kitchen? The living room? She heard the creak again, closer, coming toward her. She turned the volume back on to mask her movements, then slipped out of bed and hurried into the bathroom. It had two doors, one leading into the master bedroom where she was, another on the opposite side leading into the back hallway. It would put her behind the intruder—and she was now sure there was someone in the house. She could feel a presence. Danger was not something one simply imagines. It has a heaviness to it, and a smell. Abigail *smelled* danger; the closer it came, the more pungent the threat.

She quietly closed the bathroom door behind her, then dashed out into the back hallway. Her mind was racing. There was no time for a phone call, no time for the gun case—and what would she do with a gun she had never bothered learning to fire? That was Clarence's job, Clarence's gun. No, she needed out, out of the house, out into the darkness.

She heard him coming then, running after her. Him, her, she didn't know and had no intention of finding out. No time for car keys, no time for weapons, no time. She ran through the kitchen and saw it: an open window above the sink. Had it been left open, or unlocked? And wasn't it connected to the alarm? The alarm that *wasn't on?* What difference could it make now? She had only her nightgown on and her slippers. It was cold outside, but not yet frigid. She dashed for the front door. Throwing it open she breathed a gust of chill October air and thanked God for not abandoning her completely. Caroline and Rusty had gone for a bike ride that afternoon and left their bicycles in the driveway. Caroline's wasn't much of a bike, not one of the speedsters all the cyclists rode around this area. She had always wanted one like the bike she had as a child, and that's what Abigail grabbed now. Big, unwieldy, with handlebars that looked like antlers, a basket that never had anything in it, and *pink*. Abigail threw herself on the contraption, grateful she still knew how to ride, and pedaled furiously into the night. No lights on the roads here, maybe that would help her. But then again, no people either. No sound. No one to hear her calling for help.

# CHAPTER TWO

*Thomas West, 3ʳᵈ Baron De La Warr, died 1618.* The namesake of Delaware and the Delaware River, the only remaining undammed river in the Eastern United States. The river flows unimpeded for 330 miles from New York through Pennsylvania, New Jersey and Delaware as it makes its way to the Atlantic Ocean. Not often thought of as mighty like its cousin, the Mississippi, it regularly overflows its banks in heavy rains and leaves its high-water marks on many a home built close to the water.

Linda Sikorsky had never been very curious about the river she now lived just a half mile from. She'd crossed it many times, back and forth from Pennsylvania to New Jersey, but it was simply a particularly lovely river to her. Then, in a stroke of serendipity tinged with grief, her aunt Celeste died while watering the carnations on her back porch, in the little house she had owned in Kingwood Township, New Jersey, for some forty years. She left the house and its five acres to Linda. Not to her son Jeffrey, as the family assumed she would. Jeffrey was, by all accounts, no-account, and had moved to North Carolina with his third or fourth wife, no one was sure of the number, remaining in touch with his mother through the occasional Mother's Day card when he remembered and a visit every three to five years. That Celeste did not leave her house to him surprised no one; that she left it to Linda surprised only Linda. There really was no one else. Celeste's brother—Linda's father Pete—had been dead for thirty-five years. Celeste's own husband passed on a decade ago. Linda had been the one to visit her nearly every weekend, sometimes more often as age began to take its toll. But Celeste was determined to die on her property, if not in her bed, and it came as a relief to those who knew her when she did. That was three months ago, and after making all the arrangements that needed to be made, signing all the paperwork, and dealing with a furious Jeffrey who missed the funeral but showed up in time to be denied the keys to the house, Linda vacated her apartment in New Hope, Pennsylvania, and moved in. Alone on five acres of woods, up a road with more deer on it than cars, just a short walk and a shorter drive from the river. It had all happened so fast. Her fiancée Kirsten had not moved with her—they weren't ready to cohabitate—and now she was about to have her first visitors, here for a week of country life just seventy miles and a world away from the madhouse of Manhattan.

Autumn in the Delaware River Valley is spectacular. Its blanket of trees lining the highways and back roads turn from emerald green to a mad rush of color, with auburns and reds and yellows bursting to life as the leaves turn toward a coming winter. Linda had never imagined herself living in the woods. She had known for years that most people's ideas of New Jersey were based on late-night comedians' jokes and uninformed ridicule that assumed New Jersey's ailing cities were the sum of it. But it was called "The Garden State" for good reason: go just a short drive from Newark Airport and not far from New York City itself, and you'll find gorgeous riverbanks, forests, farms and small town life. Linda had been accustomed to living in the Valley, having served on the New Hope police force for twenty years, but she had never expected to find herself settling into a house not much bigger than a cottage on the Jersey side. She'd not had time to make it her own, and her aunt's presence was still everywhere—the furniture that had not changed since Linda was a child, the knick-knacks gathered through the years, the pots and pans, the flower beds on the back porch Celeste had been watering when death came to visit. Linda was torn about what to keep and what to change, but it would all come in time. And she wondered if Kirsten McClellan, the woman she expected to spend her life with and who was now gazing out the passenger window into the dark woods along the road, would ever want to live here with her. The engagement had happened quickly, perhaps too quickly, considering the women had only been together ten months, but Linda wanted to believe in the sincerity of Kirsten's proposal in August. The alternative—that both of them had been intoxicated with the flush of new love and now sobriety was settling in, a sobriety that might have other plans—was not something Linda wanted to think about at the moment, so she focused instead on the conversation her friends Kyle Callahan and Danny Durban were having in the back seat.

The couple Kyle and Danny had come from New York City to spend five days with her. They both insisted on calling her "Detective Linda" even though she had retired six weeks ago. She would always be Detective Linda to them: they'd met a year earlier during the murders at Pride Lodge, when Linda was the homicide detective investigating the death of handyman Teddy. Then, six months later, Linda had gone to Manhattan for Kyle's first photography exhibit at the Katherine Pride Gallery, and once again found herself in pursuit of a killer—that one especially nasty. Over the past year they had become the closest of friends, and she knew they had come to spend time with her for more than a getaway. She was in transition—leaving the police force, opening a vintage goods store in New Hope soon, and, not the least of it, moving into a small house in the woods. They wanted to support her. This much change, this quickly, can strain the strongest spirit, and Linda's was weary.

The four of them were driving home from dinner in Stockton. They'd had one of the best meals Kyle could remember ever having, enjoyed fireside in the Old Miller Inn. He and Danny had driven by the place a few times on their trips to New Hope, as they explored the surrounding area, but they had never eaten there. The meal had been exquisite, as had the company. Kyle and Danny had taken quickly to Kirsten, once she'd shown up at Kyle's photography exhibit. Her devotion to Linda was obvious, and the four of them had been talking about spending some real time together ever since.

Tonight they were driving along Route 651, up toward Lockatong Road where Linda now lived. Kyle and Danny had arrived that afternoon, after a leisurely Friday drive from New York City that included lunch and some shopping at the Flemington outlets. The day had been perfect, followed by a night of food, friendship and memories. The only thing left was to visit a short while longer at the house and settle into the attic guest room for a cozy sleep beneath a thick down comforter.

Linda was driving, chatting with Kirsten about the store she was planning to open. *For Pete's Sake*, named after her late cop father, a "vintage everything" store she'd dreamed about ever since shopping at one she loved in Doylestown, Pennsylvania, several years ago. She'd been back a half dozen times and made friends with Suzanne, the owner. Now she was getting advice from Suzanne on how to open her own store and not go out of business in six months. She had the location picked out in New Hope and had signed the lease agreement that Wednesday. So much change.

Kyle was about to ask the women what they wanted for the breakfast he'd promised to make, when the car suddenly slammed to a halt, jerking Kyle and Danny forward. Both were wearing seatbelts, and Kyle felt the belt dig into his shoulder.

"What happened?" Kyle said, worried they'd hit a deer. The animals were everywhere out here, and they often bounded out in front of cars. A collision could be fatal, and not just for the deer. But there'd been no collision. No thud, no impact.

"There," Linda said, pointing out the driver's window to the side of the road. The car was stopped, and they all followed her line of sight to the left shoulder. Just beyond it, in a pile of leaves that had accumulated in the day's wind, was a woman, next to a bicycle.

Linda quickly unfastened her seatbelt and jumped from the car, followed instantly by the others. A moment later all four of them were standing around a body—for it was a body at this point, clearly deceased—wondering what had happened. The woman was dressed in a nightgown and slippers, as if she'd fled on her bicycle at a moment's notice. The bike was what Kyle called a "Wicked Witch of the West" bike, large, with giant handlebars and a basket between them big enough to carry a small dog. The bicycle was pink with metallic flecks that shimmered in the beam of the keychain flashlight Linda used to scan the scene.

"Call 911," she said, kneeling down to examine the body.

"Already on it," Danny said, his cell phone to his ear as he reached a dispatcher and began explaining what they'd found and where they were.

The dead woman was not young; she looked to be in her sixties. One of her slippers had come off in the collision. And it was clearly a collision. Someone hit this woman and kept going.

Linda gently rolled the woman on her side for a better look. She aimed the tiny flashlight on the sad, dead face, and gasped.

"What?" said Kyle, thinking for a moment that life had been detected, that the woman's eyes had flickered or her chest had risen in a breath.

"It's Abigail Creek," Linda said.

"You know her?"

"She stopped by the house last weekend," said Kirsten. "To welcome Linda. I was here. She was a lovely woman."

"*Was*," Linda said. "She's not lovely now."

The sounds of the night grew around them. Crickets, moving things. Kyle looked up at the full moon, shining its light through the trees and onto the road. This was no accident, not in this light, not with a woman dressed as if she had been running from something.

"Who is Abigail Creek?" Danny asked.

"From CrossCreek Farm," Linda said.

"Well, that explains everything." Danny already had a knot in his gut and wished they'd had dinner at the house.

"It just might." Linda gently brushed the woman's matted hair from her face.

The four of them stood watch in the dark, waiting for an ambulance that would have no one to save.

# CHAPTER THREE

Kyle watched the sunrise through Detective Linda's kitchen window as he quietly made breakfast. He was careful not to make a sound; there were three rabbits on the side lawn, nervously looking around as they nibbled at the ground. He wished he'd brought his camera down from the bedroom but it was too late—the rabbits bounded off when they heard him set a frying pan on the stove. *Rabbit ears*, he thought.

He'd spent many nights in the countryside, most at Pride Lodge just across the river in Pennsylvania, but he had not realized how rural the area was where Detective Linda now lived. The house was on a cleared acre, surrounded by four more acres of woods. While the land around here was marked with signs saying "No Hunting," there was plenty of hunting going on in the area, but the deer were more likely to become road kill than venison.

Kyle was wearing the gray plush robe Danny gave him for his birthday. It was heavier than the October weather required, but he loved the softness of it and the oversized pockets. Beneath it he had on his travelling pajamas, so named because he only wore them when they visited people—his mother Sally in Chicago, or now, at Detective Linda's house. He slept in his boxers at home but had never been comfortable lounging around in them with anyone but Danny. He patted his belly: not bad for a man on the cusp of fifty-five. He still had all his hair, and while he was wedded to glasses he made sure they were fashionable. He and Danny were headed for their seventh year together. Lately they'd talked of marriage; at this point it was a matter of when, not if, and they would soon start the long planning phase. Both men knew it would be the only wedding they would ever have.

He took a bowl from an overhead cabinet, careful not to make too much noise. He would wait a while longer before starting the eggs, having heard the first stirrings of life from the first floor bedroom. The women were up, and Danny wouldn't be far behind. In the meantime he took his coffee and sat at the small table, the same table they'd each sat at the night before, giving statements to the New Jersey State Trooper. Her name was Jackie Overly, and she was as no-nonsense as they come. She had glanced several times at Linda and Kirsten, and Kyle wondered if she was sizing them up as family. Even in an age of marriage equality, discretion was still the order of the day. Prejudices could not be legislated away, and if, as Kyle suspected, Trooper Overly was gay, it was something she would not reveal readily, and certainly not while gathering information about a dead woman found on the road.

Who was this Abigail Creek? Kyle had tried not to listen from the living room as each of them spoke separately to Trooper Overly, but the sound carried easily in such a small house. Abigail Creek, he learned, was the matriarch of CrossCreek Farm, a large, longstanding property just a few miles up the road. There was a CrossCreek Vineyard, several lines of CrossCreek wines, and a Creek family to go with it all. He took another sip of his coffee and listened to Danny's footsteps above him in the guest room. Everyone was coming to life at the same time, even as the rabbits, crickets and birds had long been awake shouting their presence in the countryside.

Linda padded around the bedroom gathering the clothes she would wear for the day. Some of them were still in boxes—she was slow about making the house her own, as if waiting for its permission to fully claim it. Linda had been in the house many times, but never in the bedroom for more than a quick look, or following her aunt around as she spoke of one thing or another. Now she was sleeping here. It had been among her hardest tasks, to have her own bed brought in from her apartment in New Hope and her aunt's bed removed. Beds are intimate, with mattresses on which we spend a third of our lives, much of that time dreaming. Linda wondered what her aunt dreamed while she slept in this room. She knew what she dreamed for herself: a life with Kirsten, who had just slipped out to the bathroom. A business of her own that would rely entirely on her for success. An unexpected home in the woods, having no idea yet how to care for it. At forty-four, everything was changing, everything was new. It was as frightening as it was exciting.

"What are you thinking?" Kirsten said, walking back into the bedroom in her chiffon robe. She'd startled Linda, who was standing by the closet lost in memories.

*God, she's beautiful,* Linda thought. Kirsten McClellan was a very successful real estate agent, and even in her morning disarray she looked the part. Thin, short blonde hair, filling out her forty-seven years with grace and steel. They met at a New Year's Eve party the previous December and knew they were made for each other from the first hello.

"What aren't I thinking?" Linda said. "It's all so much, Kirsten. This was my aunt's bedroom, her house. I'm off the police force, I'm about to open a store, I live in the woods. And I don't know how to do any of it!"

Kirsten walked over and put her arms around Linda. Linda was several inches taller, and had always been what her mother called a "big-boned gal." Linda's hair had grown out, with Kirsten's encouragement, and it flowed in a light-brown cascade down her back.

"It's like life," Kirsten said, hugging her. "Nobody really knows how to do it until it's done. We learn on the job, Sweetie, start to finish."

"I wasn't expecting to have so much more to learn, that's all."

"Be careful what you wish for."

Linda turned around in Kirsten's arms and kissed her. "But I got what I wished for! And I don't want to be careful. I just don't want to fail."

"You're not going to fail. Put that out of your head, right this instant. And always remember, there's no failure in trying."

"The wise real estate agent speaks again."

"I read it on a cocktail napkin."

"You should be a guru or something. Guru Kirsten. You could write a book on how to live, and maybe put out a calendar with wise Guru Kirsten sayings for each day of the year. I've been collecting them, you know."

"You're silly."

Linda gently pushed her away.

"Now let's head out to the kitchen. The boys are up. I'm not sure Kyle ever went to sleep, and I smell bacon."

Kirsten stepped away, wrapping the belt around her robe. "What are you going to do today?" she said, already having an idea.

"Not sure yet."

"I find that hard to believe."

"What's that supposed to mean?" Linda said, pulling on her jeans.

"Kyle and Danny still call you Detective Linda for a reason."

"It's a term of endearment!"

"Is that what it is?"

"We won't get into trouble, I promise."

"Promise all you want," Kirsten said. "Trouble has a way of finding you. Especially when you're with Kyle. Now go ahead out and I'll be along in a minute. I'm not having breakfast in my robe, that's just for you."

Linda smiled and slipped out of the bedroom.

"It's so quiet here," Danny said, looking up from the kitchen table and out through the window. The foursome had just finished Kyle's breakfast of bacon, eggs, toast and hash browns.

"If you call a million crickets and birds that start chirping before the sun comes up 'quiet,'" Linda said. "You think an alarm clock will wake you up? Try a couple hundred finches or robins or whatever they are."

"You love it," Kirsten said. She'd dressed in her work clothes, a navy jacket over cream pants and a powder blue blouse. She was heading into New Hope soon to the real estate office that bore her name: McClellan and Powers. Her business partner was Madeline Powers, ten years her senior and the only person who could still intimidate her.

"It's not that different from New Hope," Kyle said. The trendy Pennsylvania town was only twenty minutes away.

"But it's *completely* different," Linda said. "It's country here, and I mean *country*. People think New Jersey's all Newark and Trenton. Most of it's this amazing countryside. And out here? It's not even farmland. It's woods! Deer and raccoons and woods. And I do love it."

"Amazing breakfast, Kyle," Kirsten said, setting her napkin down. "And now I'm off."

"You can't have a showing this early," Linda said. She'd been wondering if Kirsten wasn't so fond of the crickets, birds and deer, since she often headed back to the big city of New Hope soon after rising.

"We're staging a condo this afternoon. Furniture, decorations, it's all arriving in an hour. The owners are traumatized, they thought their early-modern hoarding décor was perfect, but it's been on the market for two years and that's why. We sent them on vacation for a week in Philly, put their massive crap in storage and fumigated. Now I have to sell the place before they know what hit them."

"She's the best," Linda said.

Kyle and Danny hoped it was true, that Kirsten McClellan was the best—not at selling houses and apartments, but at giving Detective Linda the love and support she believed she'd found.

"And where are the three of you off to today?" Kirsten said. She'd stood up from the table and was finishing the few drops of coffee in her cup.

"Nowhere right away," Danny said. "I've got some business calls to make later this morning."

"On a Saturday?"

"Look who's talking."

"I'm a real estate broker, we work weekends."

"And I manage a restaurant."

"Own a restaurant," Kyle corrected him. "You own a restaurant, along with me and my mother, but I'm the silent partner."

Danny and Kyle had pooled their savings and brought in Kyle's mother Sally to purchase Margaret's Passion, the Gramercy Park eatery where Danny had worked as the day manager for ten years. Last spring it was on the verge of going under, thanks to the scheming of one Linus Hern, restaurateur from hell and Danny's sworn enemy. Margaret Bowman, owner and namesake of the restaurant, ended up selling to Danny instead, and now he found himself with a restaurant on his hands. Owning and managing were two very different things, as he'd found out the last few months.

"You're welcome to be on the call with me," Danny said. "We have staffing decisions to make. I want Chloe as the new day manager, your mother wants to look around."

"I told you, I'm the silent partner. My mother does all the talking, from Chicago, no less."

"She doesn't even need a phone. You can hear her from Manhattan."

Kyle had warned Danny when he suggested bringing in Sally Callahan as the third partner. She had the extra money they needed and Danny wrongly assumed there would be few strings attached. It all happened very quickly, and Danny had not expected Sally to be quite so hands-on. Even though she lived seven hundred miles away, she discovered that owning a restaurant in New York City breathed new life into her retirement. She'd be there every day if she could, greeting customers just the way old Margaret Bowman used to. Danny thanked God Chicago was too far to commute.

"Maybe we'll go shopping later," Linda said. "And I want to show the boys the store." She was referring to the storefront in New Hope where she would soon start her business. It was empty now and being renovated, with the grand opening set for late November.

"But first?"

Linda stared at her. Damn, the woman was too good at reading her mind. Would she ever be able to do the same?

"But first," Linda said, "I thought Kyle and I could head up the road a ways."

"To extend your condolences."

"It's the right thing to do."

"Let me guess," Kyle said. He'd suspected this was coming, that it was inevitable and he might as well surrender. "We'll be visiting CrossCreek Farm."

"Abigail was kind enough to stop and introduce herself. It's only right that I pay a house call."

"You don't know anything about the Creeks," said Kirsten, "and you may not want to find out."

"She didn't deserve to die alone like that. All I want to do is offer my sympathies. They won't even know we're the ones who found the body."

"And you won't tell them."

Ten minutes later Kirsten McClellan was easing her new BMW out of the drive, careful not to let the overhanging tree limbs brush too heavily against its dark blue finish. Linda watched her from the kitchen door while Danny and Kyle cleared the table.

"I'll get the dishes," Linda said. "Just leave them on the counter. You cooked, I'll clean."

"Fair enough," Kyle said. "I want to shower and dress before we head out ... to extend your condolences."

"It might be just a terrible accident."

"Or it might be murder," Danny said, as he headed into the living room to watch the morning news. As long as he got some time away from the city he could leave Kyle and Detective Linda to their own devices.

"We'll be back in an hour," Linda said, as she rinsed off their dishes in the left sink bin. "I'll drive."

Kyle took a deep breath. He knew once they started down this road they would not turn back until they reached its end. He hoped they would not regret it as much as Abigail Creek had. Country roads could enchant you with their tree canopies and their hidden streams, and sometimes they got you killed.

# CHAPTER FOUR

CrossCreek Farm sat on thirty acres of some of New Jersey's best rural real estate. The Farm, as its inhabitants called it, had originally been the home of dairy cows, back in the 1920s when Randall Davis owned it and made his fortune in milk. It didn't have a fancy name then; everyone just called it the Davis property. Old man Davis lived alone there, having lost his wife Ruth to a deadly influenza outbreak. The couple had no children, so to the crusty, laconic farmer, his two hundred cows were his family, along with the two men who helped him maintain the farm. Those two men were Jacob Mullen and Harlan Creek, both in their thirties when everything changed and Randall went off to meet Ruth at the great dairy farm in the sky.

Jacob and Harlan could not have been more different. Jacob was six feet four and very thin. It was said if he stood sideways you'd mistake him for a post. He had long salt and pepper hair, more salt by the year even as a young man. He also had what some call Long Face Syndrome, caused by uncontrolled allergies when he was a child. It left him with a face that might go well on a horse, if horses had human faces. He was a quiet man, and by all accounts a good one. His heart, they said, was as big as his face was long. He'd been known to help a neighbor in need with his meager earnings and do without until the next paycheck. (Both men lived on the farm, in two shacks built side-by-side; room and board were part of their arrangements, so old Randall never felt bad about paying them as little as he could and still maintain a clear conscience.)

Harlan Creek was a different man altogether. He never saw himself as a farmer, let alone a dairy farmhand. He would have been perfectly fine eating the cows instead of milking them, but when he landed the job at a low point in his career as a drifter, hoping to find a log in the stream of life he could grab onto, he knew enough to play the part and see what came of it. Ten years of steady work was his payoff, a place to live, security, regular pay, and the chance to dream of something more. He was only five feet tall and had to look up whenever he spoke to Jacob, something he silently resented all the time they lived on the farm together, even though Jacob went out of his way to lean down and make Harlan feel as tall as he could without being obvious about it. Harlan was also thick—thick in the torso, thick in the legs and arms, and thick in the head. When an idea took root in his mind it had to grow until it fell away or became reality; it could not be weeded out or simply let go. And he had ideas for the Davis property. If only the old man would die and leave it to him. Which is exactly what happened.

Today CrossCreek Farm is a vineyard. Among a handful of New Jersey's best, it produces an award winning Pinot Grigio and a Sauvignon Blanc that came close to being the finest in the state. If it weren't for Blue Apple Vineyard in Salem they would take the top prize with that, too. Maybe next year, something the Creeks who currently occupied the Farm told themselves every award season. One more harvest, one more pressing, and they would be the undisputed leader in New Jersey white wines.

The Farm is just three miles up County Road 651. The house that sits like the land's master is another half mile up CrossCreek Road, which is really just a very long driveway named without humility after the landowners. When you get to the end of the driveway you find yourself at the entrance to a ranch house three times the size of most in the area. The only reason it was constructed as a single-story home was because Clarence Creek wanted to avoid ostentation. He failed.

For the Creek clan the house *was* CrossCreek Farm. The land was the vineyards, a name on a bottle of exceptional Delaware Valley wine. Were you to raze them, uproot every vine and burn them to ashes, you would still have the house, and the house is CrossCreek Farm, as inseparable from the name as it was from the family that lived in it. Built according to Clarence's own design, the house was shaped like a horseshoe. On the left side, facing the front door, were three guest bedrooms, two baths and an indoor sauna. The right leg of the horseshoe boasted the master bedroom suite, with a view through its sliding glass doors of the vineyards, a family room, kitchen, den, and temperature-controlled wine room. Immediately entering the house, down three wide marble steps, was a sunken living room, as comfortable and rustic as money could buy. Two huge couches, two matching recliners, a baby grand piano, and a well-used fireplace welcomed the many guests who came to CrossCreek Farm. Everything about the house was designed to impress.

Complementing the main house, distanced by fifty yards and two large oak trees, sits the guesthouse. It had been built as a miniature of its much larger parent, and more in the shape of a curve than a horseshoe. Also single-story, it boasted only one guest room, a kitchen made for someone who cooks, rather than someone who hires a chef, a family room and two bathrooms. No fireplace. Despite its differences, it had the appearance of being Baby Bear to Papa Bear looming over the massive lawn that connected them, and it was the first thing Kyle and Linda noticed as they rolled slowly up the driveway in Linda's beige 2006 Honda Accord.

Kyle was still feeling the weight of breakfast and wished he had skipped the potatoes. His waistline wished it too, and he reminded himself again that he needed to trim down. Now that he and Danny were serious about a wedding, his weight was an even more pressing issue: he was determined to fit into the tuxedo he'd bought for their first cruise almost seven years and thirty pounds ago.

"Nice property," Linda said, taking in the expansive lawn and the trees that ringed the front like emerald sentries, their darkening leaves fluttering in the October breeze. Everything about CrossCreek Farm was manicured, put carefully in place.

"How big do you think it is?" Kyle asked as they turned into the main circle and found a parking spot just past the three-car garage.

"Thirty acres."

"You sound sure of that."

"I looked it up," Linda said, as she unhooked her seatbelt and stepped out of the car.

She was wearing faded jeans and a blue blouse her mother had given her for her birthday. She wondered suddenly if she should have worn something more formal, more somber in light of the sudden death of Abigail Creek.

At nearly six feet, her hair tied back and her makeup kept light, Linda Sikorsky was impossible to miss. Her size and presence had served her well as a cop and then detective for twenty years, but today she didn't want to seem intimidating. Today she wanted to observe; a lot could be learned in twenty minutes, depending on who was home and how successful she was at being a compassionate bystander.

Kyle was in his usual khakis with a button-down blue pinstriped shirt, the sleeves rolled up to his elbows. He'd never much liked jeans, and he definitely didn't like the ones he fit in at fifty-four. They *looked* like old-man jeans and he just wasn't ready for that yet.

He quietly shut the passenger door, as if they'd driven into a library or a funeral parlor, which might be the case in a house of grieving family members.

"This is a vineyard?" Kyle asked as they walked to the massive front door.

"Yes, *back there*," Linda said, nodding toward the land behind the house. "You can't see it from here."

"But you checked."

"I just like to know my neighbors, that's all. I did a little research on all of them."

"To be neighborly, that's all."

"That's all."

They stood in front of the door. It consisted of three dark maple panels, with curlicues engraved up each side. The door was a piece of artistry, and when Linda rang the doorbell she was half expecting church bells to match the understated grandiosity of the house. Instead they heard ascending chimes, and a moment later footsteps on the entryway.

The door opened and a petite woman in black slacks and a gray pullover sweater greeted them. Kyle judged her to be somewhere in her late thirties, possibly forty but not much older. She had long brunette hair that flowed over her shoulders and a slightly upturned nose that reminded Kyle of Samantha Stevens on the 1960s sitcom "Bewitched." She was also in full makeup on a Saturday at 9:00 a.m.

"Hello," Caroline Creek said. "May I help you?"

"My name's Linda Sikorsky, and this is my friend, Kyle Callahan." Linda wondered if she should extend her hand. Does one shake hands with a stranger on a condolence call? She had delivered the news of a loved one's untimely death many times in her years as a homicide detective and had never once shaken hands. She decided against it. "I live a couple miles down the road, recently moved in, and Abigail Creek was kind enough to drop by and welcome me last week. I wanted to extend my condolences."

Caroline Creek stared at her and Linda immediately knew why: as fast as news spread in small communities like this, the death had only been the night before and here she was the next morning offering her sympathies.

"Well," Caroline said, forcing a smile. "I suppose somebody put it on Facebook or Twitter or some such and the next thing you know it's out there."

"Actually," Kyle said, sensing things turning in the wrong direction, "We're the ones who called 911."

"You found her?"

"I'm very sorry, but yes," Linda said. "We're the ones who discovered your mother on the roadside."

Another stare from the woman who had not budged from her position in the doorway. Then a slight smile as she said, "Oh, Abi wasn't my mother. She was my mother-in-law. Rusty Creek—her son—has been my husband for fifteen years. Where did you say you live? I know all the neighbors around here, I don't remember seeing you before."

"My aunt Celeste owned the property and left it to me."

"Celeste Dickerson, yes, I knew Celeste." Caroline relaxed suddenly. She'd known the old woman in the small house on Lockatong Road as long as she and Rusty had lived in the guesthouse. "Oh," she said. "You're her niece! The one who visited her all the time."

"Well, when I could."

"She talked about you a lot."

Linda blushed. She did not want to get sidetracked talking about herself or her aunt.

"I saw Celeste at the grocery store sometimes on Saturdays, other places around town. We had the same shopping schedule, it seemed. You're a police officer."

"Was," Linda said, wishing it hadn't come out, at least not so soon. People often went on guard when they found out the person they were speaking to was a cop. "I was a homicide detective on the New Hope police force. I retired six weeks ago."

"Congratulations! I think, if that's what you wanted to do. Please, come in. I'm sorry we have to meet under these circumstances."

Caroline Creek stepped aside and motioned Kyle and Linda into the house. The foyer was white marble and looked to be the real thing. It also shined as if someone polished it every day, but Linda doubted that someone was Caroline Creek. With a house like this, you had hired help.

"Clarence is in the living room with Rusty and Charlotte," Caroline said. She led them down two steps onto the carpeted floor, around a corner through large interior French doors and into the living room.

Like the marble entryway, the living room looked expensive and well-kept. A stone fireplace took up the back wall, and soot on the inner stones spoke of frequent use. New Jersey winters can be cold, and many of the houses here had working fireplaces. Above the fireplace was a painting of the Creek family: Clarence, Abigail, Rusty and Caroline, along with two dogs that had since passed on to doggy heaven. They were sitting in this very room and it gave the odd feeling of looking into a mirror that faced another mirror, the image repeating endlessly. Linda stared at the painting a moment and thought something was missing, or *someone*. In her research about her neighbors she recalled the Creeks having another family member, one who was not in the painting.

Kyle and Linda's attention was immediately drawn to the other people in the room. Rusty Creek, just this side of forty and noticeably overweight, sat in one of the overstuffed chairs, swallowed by it. Rusty looked like his name, over-tanned, which in October meant hours in a booth at some local tanning salon. His hair was artificially blond, and he wore black jeans with a Notre Dame sweatshirt.

Between the chair and a large green sofa sat a massive square table; too large to be called a coffee table, it had alternating brown and gold panels, as if it could be a checkerboard for someone with very expensive taste in board games.

Facing the table on its opposite side was a large green velvet couch. And on the couch sat Clarence Creek, looking stricken, holding the hand of a much younger woman who must be Charlotte.

The three of them looked up as Caroline, Kyle and Linda entered.

"Everyone, this is Linda Sikorsky and her friend Kyle."

None of them stood to welcome them. Rusty just looked at them and nodded. Clarence stared through eyes red from crying.

"Linda's new to the neighborhood, if you can call miles of countryside a neighborhood. She's Celeste Dickerson's niece, you all knew Celeste."

Finally Clarence stood up from the couch and walked over to them. He was uncommonly tall, and as he stood it had the effect of a giraffe that had been resting on the ground slowly rising to its feet. He was a thin man, probably weighing less than most men a foot shorter. He had silver hair brushed back, brown eyes and a prominent nose. He also had massive hands, and he extended one to Kyle.

"Thank you for stopping by," he said. "I understand you're the ones who found Abi on the road."

"You knew this already?" Caroline said.

Kyle and Linda glanced at each other.

"Trooper Overly told me last night when she delivered the news," Clarence said, seeing their curiosity. "She's a family friend."

Linda wondered if everyone in Kingwood Township was a family friend of the Creeks.

"Caroline and Rusty were still in the guesthouse. I didn't think to tell them. Abi was dead, what did it matter who found her?"

"I'm so sorry," Linda said. "Abigail came by the house last week to welcome me. I just wanted to extend my condolences."

"Well, I'm glad you did."

Linda kept waiting for the woman named Charlotte to say something, but she remained silent, sitting on the couch with her hands clasped in her lap. She was very pretty, though not what Linda would call beautiful. She had mid-length wavy brunette hair that brushed her shoulders above a cream silk blouse. She was wearing a light blue skirt with yellow flowers on it that hit just below the knee. She was barefoot, a very casual way to be in someone else's house. She had not been crying.

"This is Rusty, my son," Clarence said. "And this is Charlotte Gaines."

"I'd say pleased to meet you," Charlotte said, finally speaking, "but under the circumstances ..."

"I told Mother not to ride her bike on these roads," Rusty blurted. "There's no shoulder. She's not the first person to get hit around here, either. Those damn bicyclists riding all over the place in their damn Spandex and those stupid hoods."

"Helmets," Caroline said.

"Helmets, hoods, whatever. It makes them look like praying mantises on wheels. I told her not to ride on these roads. And at night? It was an accident waiting to happen. She should have gone to dinner with us. Or we should have all stayed here. It wasn't right, leaving her alone."

"Your mother wasn't feeling well," Clarence said. "It's not as if we abandoned her. She insisted on staying home. Who knows why she went riding on the road like that. Maybe she needed air. She was always going out for air."

"I just hope they find the person who did this," Charlotte said. "Accident or no, you simply don't leave someone on the side of the road you've just run down."

"Trooper Overly assures us they'll find them," Clarence said. "She said there must be evidence on the car, paint and ...." He stopped short, his voice catching; he took a deep breath, his eyes filling with tears.

Charlotte stood up quickly and took his arm, leading him back to the couch.

"Linda, Kyle, thank you so much for stopping by," she said, "but as you can see ..."

"Yes, of course," Linda said. "I just wanted to say what a friendly woman Abigail was. It meant a great deal to me to be welcomed to the neighborhood like that."

"You knew her for, what, ten minutes?" Rusty said.

His tone startled Linda.

"Rusty!" said Caroline. "Don't take your hurt out on other people, especially guests."

Linda wondered how hurt Rusty was. Maybe he was genuinely upset—it could seem inappropriate for her coming here—but maybe he was playing a part. The dynamics of the Creek family, complete with mistress in their midst, were among the more interesting Linda had seen for awhile.

"Thank you," Clarence managed to say as he eased back down on the couch, his fingers casually entwining in Charlotte's. "Now, if you'll excuse us."

"Of course."

Caroline led Linda and Kyle out of the living room. They were expecting to be shown to the front door, but instead Caroline steered them into the kitchen.

Like the rest of the house, the kitchen was oversized. It boasted two ovens and an island range that could support two or three cooks preparing a banquet. The cupboards were oak, with glass panes showing off enough dishware to feed a family of twelve.

"Would you at least like some coffee?" Caroline said, opening a cupboard and taking out three cups without waiting for an answer.

"I could use one for the road," Linda said, seeing an opportunity.

Caroline poured three cups from what smelled like a fresh pot. "Cream and sugar?"

Linda: "Black for me."

Kyle asked for cream only, which Caroline quickly provided from the double-wide refrigerator. Once their coffee was ready, she said, "Let's sit a moment on the patio. I could use some company. Besides the family, of course."

She led Kyle and Linda out through the kitchen door onto a patio. As they walked out, Linda noticed an alarm box by the side of the door. It wasn't uncommon in large houses to have more than one box, allowing people to leave and enter from different sides of the house.

The summer furniture was still out—white iron table and chairs, with a large blue umbrella to shield them from the sun.

Linda looked up at the sound of a riding lawn mower. Out about thirty yards she saw a man who looked to be in his twenties, wearing jeans and a bright white T-shirt under a red windbreaker, riding a mower the size of a small car. He was thin and his face was red from the sun, even from this distance. He waved at them. Caroline waved back.

"That's Sly," she told them. "Sly Mullen. He's been our groundskeeper since he was a boy working with his father, Carl."

"A father-son business," Kyle said.

"Oh, more than that. Sly's grandfather worked for Clarence Creek's father, and his great-grandfather Jacob worked for Harlan Creek, the original owner of the property. It goes way back. Sly does most of the big properties around here. Not landscaping, really, just yard work, upkeep and clearing, and when you've got thirty or forty acres, that's a lot of work. He's like family, or he would be if he let himself. That wave he just did is about as involved as he gets with his customers."

They watched Sly Mullen turn a corner and begin his slow ride back, mowing the lawn in a grid.

Caroline cleared her throat and said, "You being a detective and whatnot …"

"Retired."

"Yes, of course, retired. I just thought you could use a little background."

"I'm not investigating your mother-in-law's death," Linda said, knowing it was a lie and trying to understand Caroline Creek's motives for this impromptu coffee klatch.

"Charlotte Gaines is Clarence's girlfriend," Caroline continued, blowing air over her hot coffee. "Maybe I should say woman-friend at their ages. But before you draw any inferences, there was no real animosity. Between Abi and Charlotte, I mean. Abi was going to be well taken care of in the divorce."

"They were getting a divorce?" Kyle said, surprised by the information.

"Yes, but amicable. Charlotte had nothing to gain or lose if anything happened to Abi. They were *friends*, for godsake. I know that's hard to imagine, but the world's more complicated than most people like to believe. That's not the relationship I'd look at if I were a detective."

"Retired," Linda repeated.

"Yes, I'm sorry, I'll remember. Where was I?"

"Charlotte," said Kyle.

"Right. Anyway, Charlotte is a nice enough woman. She's twenty years younger than Clarence, but it's not like she's some twenty-five year old bimbo. She's forty-three! And love is love. Do I approve of it? Not at first. But I don't think Abi felt spurned, if that's the word. If it is, then there's someone else who definitely felt it, and felt it for years."

"And who would that be?" Linda asked, guessing that Caroline had brought them out here to tell them.

"Did you notice the family portrait in the living room?"

"You can't really miss it."

"It's not the entire family."

Linda knew she'd been right when she saw the painting. Someone was missing, and just as it was coming back to her from her friendly neighborhood reconnaissance, Caroline said, "Justine Creek. Their daughter. Rusty's older sister by two years, but not part of this family for the last ten."

Linda remembered now. Her aunt had spoken of the Creeks and their daughter Justine.

"What happened?" Kyle asked.

Caroline's expression darkened. "Drugs," she said under her breath, as if anyone was near enough to hear them. "From a very young age. Heroin, I think, tough it could be anything, or everything. She broke her parents' hearts. Clarence was forgiving, but not Abi. Not when she started stealing from them."

"Is she still around?" Linda asked, making mental notes of it all.

"Oh yes," Caroline said. "That's why I'm telling you. If I were going to look at anyone in this, it would be Justine. She's changed her ways, so we're told—there's no communication and hasn't been for a long time. But she's a painter now, or fancies herself one. She has a booth at the Stockton Farmer's Market and sells miniatures. I guess that's what you'd call them. Small paintings about the size of a postcard. It's her gimmick."

"Gimmick," Kyle repeated, wondering if his photography involved a gimmick. He'd had invitations to do shows after his opening at the Pride Gallery last spring, but wasn't sure he wanted anymore exposure. Photography was something he did because he loved taking pictures. Making a business of it ruined it for him in a way. No, he thought, he did not have any gimmicks, and he doubted Justine Creek did, either. She probably just liked making small paintings.

"Is the Stockton Farmer's Market one of the places you saw my aunt Celeste?" Linda asked. She knew her aunt liked going there and had been very excited when it opened.

"Yes, that's right. And I often saw Justine there, too, but we never spoke. Abi forbade any of us communicating with Justine. I don't know why she was so hard-hearted."

"But you think Justine might tell me," Linda said.

Caroline shrugged, as if to say, maybe yes, maybe no, I'm just passing it on.

"Would you like to see the vineyards?" Caroline asked.

The sudden turn of conversation gave Linda the opening she'd wanted. "Kyle and his partner Danny are only here for a few days, I think we'll pass this time."

"Time, yes," said Caroline. "There's never enough of it, and it always seems to run out. On all of us."

Before sliding her chair out from the table, Linda said, "What's this about Abigail staying home alone last night?"

"Oh, nothing, really. But the timing was terrible, wasn't it? This wouldn't have happened if she'd gone with us, or we'd stayed here. But we had reservations at the Windmill. It's one of the best restaurants in the Delaware River Valley, people come from miles away to eat there and you wait a month for a reservation. Abi wasn't feeling well so she stayed home. Clarence offered to postpone but she wouldn't have it. That was Abi, always thinking of others."

"So you all went to dinner."

"Yes."

"Including Charlotte?"

"Yes. I told you, she and Abi were friends, before Clarence and Charlotte got involved. Abi introduced them!"

"Were the Creeks swingers?" Kyle asked, immediately wishing he hadn't been so direct.

Caroline laughed. "'Swingers?' Does anyone still use that word? Does anyone still *swing*? No, no, they weren't swingers, but they did have an open relationship. At least where Clarence was concerned, and I think Abi was glad of it."

"Really?" said Linda.

"Let's just say there was no shortage of love in the marriage, but sex was another story. Abi didn't want the guilt of not having sex with Clarence the last few years. I'm saying much too much. I think Charlotte provided Abi the graceful exit she was looking for. The upcoming divorce was friendly, and as you can see Clarence doesn't hide Charlotte. Relationships can be complex."

"Yes, they can," Linda said, thinking a moment of her own.

Linda and Kyle finished their coffee, both of them wanting to leave.

"I'm sorry we had to meet under these circumstances," Linda said, rising from the table. "We can show ourselves out."

"Thank you," Caroline said. "I'm exhausted from all this. I think I'll just sit here awhile longer. We have to start planning for the funeral and all." Then, as if she'd just remembered something, she said, "The wake's tomorrow. I hope you'll come."

"I don't know …"

"Oh, please come, and don't think it's odd. Everyone's coming. Abi had a lot of friends. The whole township's likely to show up, you'll just be two more."

"Four," Linda said, "but what's four more if the whole town's here? Yes, we'll stop by."

"For Abi," said Caroline.

"For Abi."

Kyle and Linda slid their chairs in, about to leave.

"Oh," Linda said, as if it had just occurred to her, "I noticed an alarm on the door as we came through the kitchen. Did Abigail normally stay home alone with the alarm off?"

"Abi?" said Caroline. "Heavens no, she was always worried about intruders out here. She's the reason Clarence had it installed."

"Was it on when you all came home?" Kyle asked.

Caroline thought back a moment. "You know, I can't say. Clarence always turns it on and off."

28

"Well, thank you for the coffee, and the invitation for the wake. We'll be here," Linda said. They left Carline Creek sitting at the patio table and walked around the side of the house to the driveway. Kyle noticed the three garage doors were all down.

Linda, seeing him glance at the garage, said, "Yes, I'd like to get a look at those cars myself."

"Bicycle paint on a fender?"

"It would be hard to avoid, given she was hit hard enough to throw her off the road."

"But then one of the others would have seen the damage."

"Maybe not yet, it's still early, they've been dealing with this all night and morning. Or maybe there is no damage. Maybe no one in this house had anything to do with it."

As they settled back into the car, Kyle said, "She gave us a little too much information back there."

"Way too much."

"You think she's involved?"

"She certainly wants us to think someone else is."

"But they were all at dinner."

"Yes, conveniently."

"So are you still retired?" Kyle asked, fastening his seatbelt.

Linda ignored the question. She was retired from the New Hope Police Department, that was verifiable. She had not wanted to find herself chasing another murderer with Kyle Callahan, but they had all been on that road last night, and Abigail Creek had been waiting for them. So yes, she was retired, and no, she was not.

A moment later they were heading back down CrossCreek Road. Kirsten was scheduled to stop by for lunch and it was Linda's turn in the kitchen. She liked cooking. It would give her time to think about house alarms and intruders and sudden illnesses that kept a woman alone at night, far from help, where she would be easy prey.

# CHAPTER FIVE

Linda and Kyle were in the kitchen making lunch for the four of them, Linda in the lead while Kyle helped with a salad. It had been almost a year since they'd met at Pride Lodge. She hadn't expected to befriend the couple from Manhattan, but friendship is a mysterious mix of chemistry and timing, and both had been right for the three of them—especially for Kyle and Linda. Sometimes you meet someone you might not have met had the slightest thing been different, the day just a little altered, and years later you're still part of each other's lives.

"I'd love to get into that garage," Kyle said as he chopped carrots on a white plastic cutting board.

"I'm not so sure we'd find anything." Linda was kneading ground turkey in a bowl with diced mushrooms and onions, preparing to cook up turkey burgers. "They all went out to dinner last night."

"Except Abigail."

"Yes. It just doesn't fit. The whole family would have to be in on it if one of those cars was used."

"What if there wasn't any damage to the car?"

"That still doesn't answer who was driving when they were all sitting down in a restaurant ten miles away. And that bicycle was mangled. Abigail did not just ride off into the ditch. She was thrown."

"Are you saying it really was a hit-and-run? That none of them had anything to do with it?"

"I don't believe that at all. We walked into a family web there this morning. We just have to determine which of them is the spider."

Danny had been in the living room on yet another call about the restaurant. He'd had second thoughts about buying the restaurant with

Kyle's mother as a partner. While she nearly always deferred to Danny's decisions, she enjoyed making him fight for them.

Kyle heard Danny swear as he hung up the phone and walked into the kitchen.

"She's impossible," Danny said, taking a seat at the small kitchen table. "What am I going to do when she's *legally* my mother-in-law? This could be a deal breaker, Kyle."

"I hate to say I told you so."

"If you hated it you wouldn't say it."

Kyle had cautioned Danny against borrowing money from Sally Callahan when Danny first proposed his plan to save Margaret Bowman and the business. While she lived in Chicago, she was not the type to be a silent partner in anything, and Kyle's warning had come true. Sally had spent the six months since they'd purchased the restaurant meddling in every detail. For years she'd been content to visit Kyle and Danny and eat at least one meal at Margaret's Passion without the slightest critical comment on the venerable eatery. But since becoming an owner she had been finding things she thought needed improvement, which she phrased as "just some suggestions." Danny soon discovered that for Sally Callahan, suggestions were meant to be taken. It resulted in the first real friction Danny had with her during his years with Kyle.

"She gave in on hiring Chloe as the day manager, but she wants to interview the new chef applicants," Danny said. "By Skype."

"Is that a hardship?" Kyle asked.

"It's theater, is what it is. She doesn't know anything about running a restaurant. I wish Chef Jeff wasn't leaving, I begged him, but his father's sick in Denver, the timing could not be worse. She just makes me feel so ..."

"Put-upon."

"Well, yes. I was the day manager there for ten years, effectively running the place. I trust my instincts when it comes to hiring people, and I don't need your mother's Kabuki."

"Just her money," Kyle said, chopping the last of the carrots.

Linda had been listening and reserving comment. She knew better than to inject herself into the conversation. She had only met Sally

Callahan once, at Kyle's photography exhibit. She'd liked her very much, but she had pegged Sally as a tough character.

"How's Margaret?" Linda asked.

"She's fine," Danny said. "Eighty-two next month and sharp as ever. But she's at an age where the finish line is in sight and she's thinking of an exit strategy."

"Assisted living?"

"Florida. She has a younger sister who lives in Coral Springs. Rebecca is her name. She almost has Margaret convinced they should move to a senior community together."

Danny's mood darkened. He would hate to see Margaret move away, and he knew she would prefer to live out her life in the apartment she'd shared with her late husband Gerard, above the restaurant she had worked thirty years to create and sustain. But time was an implacable foe and never lost. Danny knew it would not be long before Margaret Bowman packed her things and headed south. It would also put the restaurant in a precarious position, since she would likely sell the building. Danny, Kyle and Sally had bought only the restaurant. Would a new owner let them stay? Danny was unclear on the legalities. He would have to look into them soon.

Kyle glanced out the small window over the sink and saw Kirsten pulling into the driveway. He hadn't had a chance yet for a heart-to-heart with Linda about how it was going; not what she would tell most of her friends, but how it was *really* going: was Linda happy? Was their relationship flowering? Would they ever live together, let alone marry? He knew Linda hoped this was the one and that she secretly worried it might not be. Kirsten McClellan was strong-willed and successful. She had lived as an out lesbian all her adult life, and no doubt had enjoyed a few relationships on her way to forty-seven. She may be Linda's first love, but Linda was surely not hers.

The four of them ate on the back patio. Late October was gorgeous in rural New Jersey. Linda's property was surrounded by trees that were now clothed in rich, dark colors as more of their leaves fell each day. Dark oranges, reds and yellows. The back yard needed mowing, its grass a good six inches tall. The patio itself was small, just large enough to accommodate a wrought-iron table and four chairs, plus a few planters Kyle knew Linda would fill with flowers in the spring.

Kirsten had driven over from New Hope after staging the condo she was trying to sell. She had spent years building up her very successful real estate business, and the work habits she had needed as a young agent were still with her. Linda considered her a workaholic, and it was one of the things she wasn't happy with. Linda had encouraged her to slow down, telling her that working seven days a week and being available for clients nearly round the clock was not necessary anymore. It was as if Kirsten were running from a poor past she believed she could never escape, no matter how much money she had. Linda had slowed down and was about to spend her days sitting at a cash register, talking to customers and getting to know as many of them as she could. She'd moved to her aunt's house in the woods. She wanted to savor the passing years, having been aware since her father's senseless death that life can end in an instant. It was a conversation Kirsten always managed to avoid.

"So what did the two of you discover on your condolence visit?" Kirsten asked when they were settled in for lunch.

"I'm offended by the implication," Linda replied. "We were there for a grieving family."

"Everyone at this table knows better," said Kirsten. "I'm sure you honestly feel for them and think this was a tragedy, but you were there with your eyes and ears open."

"You're right," Kyle said. "It was a fishing expedition, and the fish bit. At least one of them. Caroline Creek, that's the daughter-in-law, married to son Rusty. She was very forthcoming."

"Forthcoming about what?" Danny asked.

"She pointed us in the direction of Justine Creek," said Linda, "the family's black sheep and someone with issues, at least between herself and her mother."

Kyle added, "She also wanted us to know that the mistress ..."

"Mistress?"

"I guess they still call them that. The 'other woman,' whatever's in use now. Charlotte Gaines. She looks about twenty years younger than

Clarence, and she's obviously comfortable being in that house, around that family. They all seem to know each other very well."

"Except Justine," Linda said.

"It sounds a little weird to me," said Danny, "if not creepy. Abigail knew about this?"

"Yes!" Linda replied. "She introduced Charlotte and Clarence. The divorce proceedings are amicable, whatever that means."

"It means—"

"I know what it means. But it can be in degrees. Amicable as in, we'll still speak to each other from time to time, we have the children together. Or amicable as in, you've been my best friend for forty years and you'll always be my best friend."

"Or amicable as in, let's have a three-way," Kirsten offered, getting looks of surprise from the others. "What? What's wrong with a three-way? Or does that only turn you on when they're all twenty?"

Linda wondered what Kirsten's experience of three-ways was. "It's a peculiar situation all around," she said. "Abigail and Clarence are divorcing. I'd guess Charlotte will be moving in soon, if she hasn't already. The son and daughter-in-law seem perfectly comfortable with all of it."

"Somebody wasn't comfortable with it," Kyle said.

"That's right. Somebody was uncomfortable enough to chase down—not just run down, remember she was wearing her nightgown, she was a woman in flight—chase down and plow into Abigail Creek with their car."

"Or maybe none of them did it," Danny said, throwing cold water on their speculation.

They finished their lunch, changing the subject to the fall weather in Kingwood Township and the glorious colors all around them in the trees, the cool temperatures that would soon become cold with winter's arrival.

When they finished, Kirsten announced she had to head back to the open house, the lookiloos would start arriving soon. She said she would see them in New Hope for dinner—they'd made a reservation at Georgia Darling's, one of the finest restaurants in Pennsylvania, and one of the most expensive. Kyle had made them promise to eat at the house the next few nights. As much as he loved all the fine shops and restaurants in the area, it would be a strain on the budget.

Watching Kirsten pull out of the driveway, Kyle said, "Does she ever stop?"

"Just long enough to sleep," Linda said.

Kyle could tell in her voice that Kirsten's insistence on working constantly was a problem for Linda. Young love, he thought. Or maybe it should be first love, since Linda and Kirsten had not been young for a few years. New relationships are fraught with learning curves and bumps as the couple got to know each other—each other's habits, desires, routines and quirks. He fervently hoped it would last, and he wanted to be a mentor of sorts—a love mentor—if he could.

"If you ever want to talk," he said.

"I'll let you know."

Danny had gone back into the living room and was reading the New York Times on his iPad. He had promised himself he would not do anymore work for the rest of the weekend, and had turned his phone off. He knew when he turned it on again there would be dozens of emails and a text message or ten, but he was trying to slow down. As he approached fifty-seven he had become more aware of time passing; and not just passing, but flying more quickly each year. He wanted to experience as many days as he could. He'd already spent too much time today on the phone with Sally Callahan, fretting over business decisions he could not do anything about until they got back to Manhattan.

"What's next on our itinerary, Detective Linda?" Kyle asked as they finished cleaning up.

"Have you ever been to Stockton?" she asked. "I know you've driven through it."

"We've never stopped. It's only a couple blocks long. But as I recall there's a farmers market there."

"Yes there is, and I think you might enjoy walking around it, they have great pastries, handmade soaps ..."

"Miniature paintings."

"Those, too."

They finished up the dishes and got ready to head out again. Soon they would be perusing the stalls at the Stockton Farmers Market, with one in particular on Linda's mind. She wondered, as Kyle told Danny to grab his jacket and meet them at the car, if Justine Creek was enough of a black sheep to commit murder. And not just any murder, but the murder of the woman who had brought her into this world and then, years later, turned her away.

# CHAPTER SIX

Stockton, New Jersey, was at most a fifteen minute drive from Linda's house. Located along the Delaware River north of Lambertville, it was first known as Reading Ferry and later as Howell's Ferry. Eventually the name was changed to Centre Bridge Station to match the name of the post office and hamlet on the Pennsylvania side of the river. Finally it was renamed Stockton, in honor of U.S. Senator Robert Field Stockton, who had been central to the creation of the Delaware and Raritan Canal.

The small town looks today much as it did in the eighteenth century. It continues to be dominated by the Stockton Inn, established in 1710 as a private home and converted into an inn in 1832. The Inn remains a popular restaurant, drawing diners from far and wide who come to enjoy its history and high-quality food.

Immediately perpendicular to the Inn is Bridge Street, aptly named because it leads directly to the Stockton-Centre Bridge crossing that allows cars and pedestrians to meander over the Delaware River into Pennsylvania. It's a bridge Linda Sikorsky had driven over hundreds of times, coming from New Hope to visit her aunt Celeste. On the Jersey side, a single block of businesses had served the community for many decades. One relative newcomer, the Stockton Farmers Market, opened its doors three years ago and was now a thriving bazaar of organic food merchants, a fish monger, tea sellers, and various other booths run by merchants looking to sell their wares to the steady flow of customers swelling Stockton's population on the weekends.

"Parking's a challenge," Linda said, as she turned onto Bridge Street with Kyle in the passenger seat and Danny in the back. "But that's a good thing. The Market's only been here a few years and boy, has it brought the business in."

Danny was still looking out the back window at the Stockton Inn. It stood like a tired but elegant old sentry, staring directly down Bridge Street toward the river. He'd seen it on past trips around the area and had always wanted to try their food; perhaps they could on this trip.

Linda followed a slow-moving line of cars, turned into the alley and managed to find a parking spot in the back after waiting five minutes for someone to pull out.

"Place is hopping," Kyle said as they walked to the back entrance.

"It's been great for the community," Linda replied. "It brings in as many tourists as locals."

They walked into the market and were immediately greeted with the smells: flowers, produce, soaps, herbs, and cooking. There were at least a hundred people milling among the vendors, picking up items to check their prices, sampling tiny cupcakes and spoons of frozen yogurt in October's special flavor—pumpkin spice.

The three of them made a slow circle around the market with Linda in the lead. Danny wondered if she was really interested in what was being sold, or if she was aiming for the appearance of nonchalance. They had come here to see one vendor, with one intention in mind, and he wasn't sure why they were wandering such a roundabout way.

After stopping at what seemed every single booth and stall, Linda led them to a large wooden table that had a half dozen small paintings displayed on it, with several more on an easel behind it. A woman sat in a chair behind the table watching all the customers ambling through the vast open space. She had her hands folded in her lap. Not reading a magazine, not looking at a smartphone or tablet. Just sitting serenely, staring out at the crowd. She was wearing a long brown velvet skirt and a beige blouse that flowed down over her waist. Her auburn hair ran halfway down her back, knotted into a single thick braid. Her face was narrow, her eyes a warm chocolate, and Kyle immediately saw the resemblance to Clarence Creek. Tall, thin, slightly angular. She was clearly her father's daughter.

"Anything special you're looking for?" Justine Creek said to Linda as she scanned the paintings on the table. She accompanied the question with an easy smile.

"I just moved into a small house in Kingwood, inherited from my aunt, and I'd like to make it mine, you know? Not so much it isn't *hers* anymore, but enough that it feels like home."

"I completely understand."

"I think some original paintings would be nice."

"These are great for small spaces. Kitchens, bathrooms, above a desk."

The paintings were miniatures of what you might expect to find on canvases many times their size. Landscapes and portraits, mostly, with an expressionist element.

Linda was admiring them when her gaze suddenly froze on one of the paintings.

"That's outside my house," she said, startled. "Lockatong Road. I mean, *right outside* my house."

"If that's your house, then I knew your aunt," Justine said. "Celeste. She came here almost every Saturday, very nice woman. She never bought a painting, but she invited me for lunch sometime, and I accepted. I loved the view down that road, especially when the leaves were full. Dark, luscious green. It's like looking into a dream. I asked her if I could make a painting of it."

"I think that's one you have to have," Kyle said. He was impressed by Justine Creek's talent, and he didn't think it was the work of someone with an ongoing drug problem. This kind of art, with its demand for precision, patience and persistence, simply didn't fit with the picture of a woman disowned by her family for addictions and thievery.

Danny had wandered off to talk to an African-American couple selling custom teas at a booth nearby. He was pleased to see the couple in what was an otherwise very white environment, but he was also on the lookout for new items for Margaret's Passion. One-of-a-kind teas might be something to consider. Now that he owned the restaurant as well as ran it, he wanted to make some changes and additions—with Margaret's blessing, of course. (He would not be asking Sally Callahan for her opinion of the teas.)

Linda decided to take a risk, knowing they couldn't linger long once she bought the painting. "I'm sorry about your mother, by the way," she said, discreetly watching Justine for her reaction, any telltale signs of guilt or involvement in the death.

"Yes," Justine said. "My father called me this morning. I suppose I'm sorry, too."

"Suppose?" Kyle said.

Justine stared at him a moment, but not angrily. It was more an expression of weariness, as if the whole matter of her family, its conflicts and dysfunction, was simply something she had no time for anymore.

"My mother and I didn't get along and haven't—hadn't—spoken for several years. She came here sometimes, of course, everyone does. But we didn't speak. Why am I telling you this? And why are you asking?"

Linda could tell Justine was becoming suspicious and decided transparency was the best approach.

"We're the ones who found your mother. Last night, on the side of the road."

"So you coming here, buying a painting of the road outside your house, is not coincidence."

"Coincidence, no," Kyle said, hoping they could seize the moment before Justine decided to say nothing. "Serendipity, yes."

"There's a difference?"

"I had no idea there was any connection between you and my aunt," Linda offered.

"And I had no idea you found my mother dead on the side of the road. Now what is it you want to know? That's why you're really here, isn't it? Are you a reporter? Are you looking for a story to sell? And what is your name, by the way? You knew mine before you got here."

"Linda. Linda Sikorsky. This is Kyle Callahan, and that man over there at the tea booth is his partner Danny Durban. They're visiting for a few days."

"Linda was a homicide detective for the New Hope Police Department until six weeks ago," Kyle said.

"Ah, now that's serendipitous," Justine said with a rueful smile. "A homicide detective finds my mother dead on the road. Maybe there are angels after all. I think it's time for me to take a short break and have some coffee out front. Join me, we'll have more privacy there."

Kyle looked around at the milling crowd. "Your paintings will be safe?"

"Oh yes. Clara keeps an eye out for me." She waved to an elderly woman directly across the room selling baked goods. "We do that for each other. I'll just put my 'Back in 15 Minutes' sign out and we can go."

Five minutes later the four of them were sitting at a small round metal table in front of the market. This short stretch of Bridge Street had always been the center of Stockton's commercial district, if a block or two can be called that, and the Farmers Market had brought it to vibrant life after years of stagnation.

They had all purchased coffee at the coffee shop that was adjacent to, and part of, the larger indoor market. Danny treated himself to a cappuccino, while Linda and Kyle had straight coffee and Justine drank ginger tea.

"I know you came here to see me," Justine said, sipping from her to-go cup, the tea bag still immersed with its string hanging over the side. "So let's just be upfront about it all. I can get back to selling my artwork and you can get back to your Saturday."

Kyle was beginning to like this Creek family black sheep. She seemed confident and exceptionally frank, and it struck him, observing her directness, that if she had killed her mother she would probably just come out and say it.

Linda said, "Caroline Creek was telling us …"

"Of course she was," Justine said. "Caroline likes to tell people things."

"I take it there's no love lost between the two of you," said Kyle.

"There was never any love found. Caroline Creek is an opportunist. She married my halfwit brother to become a Creek, with everything that entails."

"And what does it entail?" Linda asked.

"Property, assets, money, envy, greed, treachery. Should I continue?"

"I get the picture. What about your relationship with your mother?"

Justine took another slow sip of tea, thinking about her response.

"There wasn't much of a relationship," she said. "And what there was, was … unpleasant. I had some troubles, years ago. I took advantage of my father's generosity. I fell into the wrong company, did bad things to my body and my mind. Oh, and I stole from them. That was what she never forgave. I took some heirlooms that had belonged to her mother and her grandmother and traded them for heroin and cocaine. Is that enough of an answer?"

"You're clean now?" Danny asked. He'd had some experience with addicts over his years in the restaurant business.

Justine sighed. Her state of sobriety had been questioned many times before, including by her own family. "Yes," she said. "Six years now. Not a drop, not a toke, not a snort."

"So why not reconcile with your family?"

"Oh, I have. But only with my father. Abigail—Mother—she refused to believe I'd changed. And she always loved a good grudge."

"But no grudge against Charlotte Gaines, the woman taking her place," Kyle said.

"Is that what you were led to believe? Interesting. But it's an interesting family, I'll give the Creeks that. As for her reaction to knowing my father stayed in contact with me all this time, she was furious"

"Really?" said Linda.

"Yes. We email, sometimes we talk on the phone. He was even putting me back in the will. I was going to be an heiress again." At that she laughed.

"But your mother—"

"Threw a fit, yes. Several fits."

Linda was thinking it all through as she listened. If Abigail Creek was that opposed to her daughter being brought back into the fold, could she have convinced, or somehow forced, Clarence to leave their daughter out of his will? Would such a thing have been a threat to Justine? For all her calm and cool, there was a lot of property and money at stake. Linda knew from inheriting her aunt's house while

Celeste's son had been cut out that money and family can make for an ugly situation.

"I wouldn't kill her for it," Justine said, as if she had read Linda's mind. "I've done just fine without the Creek fortune, and I will keep doing fine. I have no idea if I'm in the will or not. And I don't care."

"Why do you suppose Caroline was so keen on pointing us in your direction?" Kyle asked.

"So you wouldn't look at her husband!" she said, and chuckled. "Russell has a fondness for booze—something my mother didn't seem to put in the same category as my drugs of choice—and a gambling habit that hasn't gotten him killed yet only because my father bails him out. Although I'd have to say Rusty doesn't really have the brains for anything too complicated."

"Running someone off the road isn't very complicated," Danny offered.

"Ah," said Justine, "but I bet they all had an alibi. Now that takes some planning." She finished the last of her tea. "If you'll excuse me, I really do need to sell some paintings."

"I'd like the one of the road outside my aunt's—my house," Linda said.

"Excellent. Come on in and I'll wrap it up for you."

As they stood from the table, Linda said, "Where would you start, Justine? If you were asking around, discreetly. As an outsider who's also an insider, maybe you could give us some advice."

Justine thought about it a moment. "Sly," she said. "Sly Mullen."

"The groundskeeper?" Kyle asked.

"He's really more of a lawn guy, flowerbeds and whatnot. His father used to do a lot more, but I think Sly's not a servant at heart. The rich folks around here have large yards, if you haven't noticed. And they like having servants."

"Why would you suggest we speak to him?"

"It's the people you don't notice," Justine said, "who notice everything. Sly Mullen, like his father and his grandfather before him, is always there in the background, pulling a weed, trimming a hedge, and watching. I'd have a talk with Sly."

Kyle definitely liked the woman now. He had no reason to judge her based on her past addictions and bad behavior. She had turned her life around, and in the process she had saved a very intelligent, forthcoming and talented woman … herself. He wanted to take another look at her paintings, thinking he might like something new for their apartment in Gramercy Park.

"I'll wait out here," Danny said, still sipping his cappuccino as Justine, Linda and Kyle headed back into the market. He knew Kyle was going to buy a painting and he would just as soon not know the price.

# CHAPTER SEVEN

New Hope, Pennsylvania, is located approximately halfway between Philadelphia and New York City, along the route of the Old York Road, once the main highway between the two cities. Travelers would stay overnight here and be ferried across the Delaware River the next morning, where they would continue their journey. Route 202 that passes just north of town still bears the name York Road, and the original route is now known as Bridge Street, the very street Linda, Kyle and Danny drove down as they made their way from Stockton. Originally called Coryell's Ferry, after the owner of the ferry who took people across the river from one state to the other, the town was renamed after a large fire in 1790 burned down several miles in the area and its reconstruction was considered a "new hope" for residents.

"They could have called it 'New Beginning' I suppose," Linda said, as she looked for a parking spot on a side street off Main.

There were three primary streets in New Hope: Main, Bridge and Mechanic. Main Street is considered prime business real estate. It's where you'll find many of the shops and restaurants that attract tourists year round, including the famous Georgia Darling's where they were meeting Kirsten for dinner. It's also where Linda had found an available storefront for her vintage shop.

Difficult economic times had been upon the country for several years now, and New Hope had not been spared. Some of the shops Kyle and Danny enjoyed visiting just a year ago were no longer in business, including Heaven's Scent, where Danny liked buying handmade soaps that could be found nowhere else, and two art galleries that had offered affordable art. One of the galleries, Fine Print, had included photography and sold two of Kyle's original photos out of a dozen they had displayed. The rest were shipped back to Manhattan with a gracious but very sad note saying the gallery was closing at the end of July. It was now October and the store remained empty.

Linda found a spot a half block from Main and they all walked downhill to the thoroughfare. It was late afternoon and chilly, but there were plenty of people walking both ways along the street. Cameras and smartphones were plentiful as everyone took photos of the quaint town. New Hope is known for its arts community and has a bohemian feel, with writers, painters, bikers and tattooed ice cream vendors all intermingling. Bucks County Playhouse stands tall by the river and for decades produced Broadway-caliber shows with some of the finest talent brought in from New York. The Playhouse nearly went under and was shuttered for awhile, but investors stepped in to save it, allowing one of the area's icons to survive.

Linda led them two blocks up Main Street from where they'd parked and there, on the right, was an empty store with the name Candy Apple's still visible on the front glass.

"Evelyn Apple," Linda said, noticing Kyle read the name of the now-defunct candy store. "That's really her last name. Unfortunately we live in a society where eating candy is going the way of smoking."

"Oh, yes," Kyle said. "They'll ban it soon, at least in public places. I'm surprised it's still legal in New York City."

Linda fished in her purse for the door key. She had signed a lease three days before. The man who owned the building had given her the key and said, "Good luck," with a look that said she would need it.

"Borys is a great guy," Linda said, referring to her new landlord. "Borys Pavlenko. Ukrainian. I have no idea of his history or how he came to own a building in New Hope, but he's a sweetheart. He was terribly sad when Evelyn couldn't make a go of the candy shop, but he has bills to pay, too."

The shop had been gutted, leaving only three large cases that had held a dizzying variety of candy, none of it quite enticing enough in an age of aerobics and sugarless, fat-free food to keep the place in business.

Linda flipped on the lights as they entered. "I knew Evelyn from the candy store. She tried. I'll try. It's all you can do."

"It's a big space," Danny said. The three of them stood in the center of a large open room, empty except for the display cases. A lonely vacuum cleaner stood against one wall, and a curtain hung over a door leading to a back area.

"Bathroom and a storage closet behind the curtain," Linda said. "The cases will come in handy, and I've been shopping on the weekends for some vintage cabinets—I won't say antique, I can't afford that. But it will be a vintage store. I've also gone to some auctions with Suzanne, my mentor from Doylestown. She's teaching me the ropes of finding things people want to buy in stores like ours. Luckily she's too far away to consider me competition."

Linda had imagined opening the store for several years, well before she finally decided to retire from the police force. She'd done her time there and left with a comfortable pension. She knew she'd see her old colleagues around town and several had already offered to help put the store together if she needed them. She couldn't really say which came first: the name of the store, or the idea for it. *For Pete's Sake* had been tumbling around in her mind forever, she just didn't know what she would use it for. Like becoming a cop, it was a way to keep her father alive. Losing him when she was just a child remained the deepest scar she would ever have, and one that could not go away, nor would she want it to. She had idolized her father, always a good and heroic man in her mind. She wanted to believe he had somehow watched over her all these years, and that he would be her first customer in a shop named after him. She had no idea what a ghost would be interested in, but she knew her father would come in on a breeze the first moment of the first day she was open for business.

"You'll be close to Kirsten," Kyle said. "She can't live too far from here, New Hope's not that big a place."

"About a mile away," Linda said. The subject of her relationship with Kirsten wasn't something she was ready to discuss, so she changed the subject. "Why would a man who always turns the alarm on leave his wife at home alone with it off?"

"Unless they own guns and he thought she could protect herself," Danny said.

"Then why have the alarm at all?"

"To protect the house when no one's home."

"But someone was home," Kyle said. "Abigail Creek."

"Alone, in her nightgown," Linda said. "But she wasn't supposed to be. She was supposed to go to dinner with them. Maybe he forgot she wasn't coming!"

"Then he would have turned it on."

"What if he did," Danny said, "and someone else turned it off? Maybe someone who forgot her purse and went back into the house."

"Or his flask," Kyle said, recalling Rusty Creek's belligerence at the house. Kyle pegged him as a man who liked a drink, confirmed just an hour ago by his sister Justine.

"Who can you ask?" said Danny. "They were all there at the time. One of them knows who sat in the front seat, who sat in the back, and who went back into the house, if any of them did."

"We can ask the same person who was so eager to tell us everything else she wanted us to know," Linda said. "Caroline Creek."

"A wake seems like the wrong place to ask questions like these."

Linda smiled. "Oh, I think that may be why she invited us."

Danny glanced at his watch. It was quarter past six and they had a six-thirty dinner reservation.

"We should head out," Danny said. "We don't want to keep Kirsten waiting."

*Why not?* Linda wondered. *She keeps me waiting … and waiting.*

"Your father would be very proud of you," Kyle said as they left the store, Linda locking the door behind them.

"I like to think so. I like to think he sees me from somewhere."

"In here." Kyle placed his hand above his heart. "He sees you from in here."

Linda nodded, dropped the keys back in her purse, and led them toward the restaurant two blocks away.

# CHAPTER EIGHT

Kyle had to be careful not to hit his head on the ceiling. The attic guest room was a comfortable but tiny A-shaped room that held a bed, dresser, television, and several low tables along walls that only went up three feet before beginning to slope to a point. A desk was placed against one wall, just tall enough to fit against it and, as desks went, impractical: someone could sit there and write or read, but nothing useful could fit on the desk.

"I love this room," Kyle said. It reminded him of his grandmother's attic in Pontiac. His father was raised in Michigan, and until Kyle was sixteen and his paternal grandparents moved to Arizona, he would make the drive with his parents to Pontiac every summer for a week's stay. Grams Callahan loomed large in his childhood. He remembered all the worlds he'd imagined upstairs in her attic, its dusty beams transformed in his fantasies into castle hideaways and haunted cabins. There were no beams in Detective Linda's house, but the effect was the same. He was a little boy again, forever at play in his imagination.

Danny was on the bed, the bedspread pulled up over him. "I thought heat rose to the top," he said, shivering slightly in the evening chill.

"She said we could use the space heater."

"I don't think so. Too many stories of fires started with those things. I'd rather be cold than dead."

"In the woods."

"Exactly."

Kyle thought a moment. "I don't think Kirsten likes it here," he said." Kirsten had not come back with them after dinner.

"Maybe she just likes her space. There are couples like that, you know. Lots of them. It's not like they're both just starting out. People get set in their ways, they have their own homes or apartments. It's whatever works for them."

"But what if it only works for one of them?" Kyle slid into bed bedside Danny. The small television was on low, some sitcom rerun playing like white noise in the background. "What if Kirsten never wants to live together? Can you really marry someone and not live with them?"

"You're worried they're not going to make it."

"I don't know if I'd put it that way. I just know Linda had such high hopes. And they seem so suited to each other."

The women did appear well matched. The four of them had eaten an amazing meal at Georgia Darling's, entertained throughout by a very well-seasoned waiter who knew how to work his customers. He had them laughing and talking through their four courses, as much to him as to themselves.

"We were well suited to each other," Danny said, smiling as he remembered hitting it off with Kyle from that very first accidental meeting. They had both been at the Katherine Pride Gallery for a photography show. The photographer was a friend of Kyle's, and Kate Pride and her husband had recently eaten at Margaret's Passion. Kyle was there in support of his friend and Danny was there to keep two happy customers coming back. Danny came around a corner with a glass of wine and literally bumped into Kyle. Ooops, so sorry. The two men looked at each other, and seven years later they were talking of marriage.

"I know I have to let it go," Kyle said, turning on his Kindle. He enjoyed reading for twenty minutes or so before sleep. It had worked for him all his life, more effectively and reliably than any sleep aide. Nothing made him quite as tired as five pages of a good novel.

"She's going to be fine. She's forty-four years old. She was a cop for twenty years. Her father was gunned down when she was eight, for godsake. You think she can't navigate a relationship and survive if it hits the rocks?"

"Of course she can. I just want her to be happy."

Danny adjusted the bedspread. "I'm not looking forward to this wake tomorrow. Isn't it kind of strange that we're here for vacation and we're going to a wake?"

"Don't you want to know who killed her?"

"No! For one thing, trying to find out who a killer is can get you killed. And secondly ... we're on vacation!"

"Oh, so if someone had a heart attack on the sidewalk in front of you you'd just step over them and say, 'Sorry, I'm on vacation.'"

"She didn't have a heart attack. She was already dead."

"You're cold, Danny Durban."

"I'm not cold. I'm realistic."

"So do it for Detective Linda. She has so much going on, this could be a good distraction for her."

"Great idea. Something to keep her mind off retiring and being in a difficult relationship: a dead woman with a dangerous family. I highly recommend it."

Kyle set his Kindle aside and stared at Danny. "You're jealous, that's what this is."

"I am not."

"You *are*. I just realized it. It bothers you when I get together with Detective Linda. You're not the focus of my attention for a few days."

"You're too scattered for anyone to be the focus of your attention," Danny said. "I just miss the days when all you did was take pictures, read books and cater twenty-four hours a day to Imogene."

Kyle's boss, Imogene Landis, was a television reporter for a Japanese cable show. Her career had been on life support, with Imogene reduced to English-language financial reporting for the 3:00 a.m. Tokyo crowd, when she covered the Pride Lodge murders and became a cult sensation. In the year since, she had been reassigned to cover New York City for the same audience, who found her endlessly amusing. She didn't care; she was in the big time again, in a small way. It had led to a few job offers, none of which she'd yet taken, something Kyle was grateful for. It might mean Imogene leaving New York and the thought made him sad. Life without Imogene would be so much less colorful.

"That won't be an option much longer," Kyle said. "The Imogene part, anyway. She'll move on eventually, I know she will."

"You would want her to, Kyle. She's like us, she hasn't been young for a couple decades and this is probably her last shot at semi-stardom."

"But she is a star!"

"To a bunch of people in Tokyo who think she's a comedy act. She knows that, she's not stupid. She finally has a stone to step on, you have to accept it when she does."

"She asked me if I'd go with her if she moved." Kyle hadn't told Danny about this until tonight.

"I could never leave Manhattan."

Kyle smiled. "I said she asked *me*."

"So go. I'm sure there are lots of murders to solve in San Francisco or Seattle or Akron."

"I'm not going anywhere without you. What are we watching?" He nodded at the television, where a rerun of The Andy Griffith Show was on.

"Aunt Bee is about to share some of her Aunt Bee-isms."

"Frances Bavier was her name," Kyle said. "She spent her last years as a recluse in a small dark house, with a Studebaker in the garage with four flat tires."

"How do you know these things? Better yet, *why* do you know them?"

Kyle shrugged. He was an information sponge, if this sort of trivia could be called information. "Let's listen," he said, taking the remote and turning up the volume. He wanted to think of something else, tired of discussing Detective Linda, dead bodies and the possible departure of his irritating, demanding, beloved boss. Life goes on, he thought. Unless you're Abigail Creek riding a bicycle on a dark country road.

Linda could hear the television in the attic room above her. She had only her white noise machine to fill the silence of the empty house in the woods. In this case it helped muffle the men's voices above her. She was very glad of the company, and especially happy to have Kyle and Danny visiting. They were her only visitors since moving in except Kirsten, and where was she tonight? In her own home, her elegant condominium in

New Hope, sparsely furnished, costly art on the walls. Had she been fooling herself all these months? Linda wondered. Whatever made her think Kirsten McClellan, high-powered, well-established Bucks County real estate broker, would be happy with someone like her? She was a cop, now retired. She lived in a little house on the Jersey side, with deer for neighbors and the deafening sound of crickets to surround the house in summer. We're so different, Linda thought, tossing side to side in bed. *What was I thinking?*

The two women met at a New Year's Eve party ten months earlier. Detective Linda Sikorsky had just officially come out and the party was the first she had ever been to populated mostly by lesbians. Her colleague, Officer Steve Fischer, had a gay sister and suggested Linda reach out to her for support and to start creating some kind of community for herself. Coming out at forty-four was not easy. It wasn't that Linda had ever rejected herself; she had honestly feared getting close to anyone, certainly not close enough to love. The death of her father had thrown her and her mother's lives into turmoil. An eight-year-old girl decided then and there never to love that fiercely again, and that meant never getting close enough to someone for that to happen. Acknowledging who she was, who she was attracted to, would have opened that door and she had kept it closed and locked all her life. Until she met Kirsten McClellan.

There were no obvious signs of trouble in their relationship. The women did not fight, not really. Linda had just been painfully aware of Kirsten's independence. Being completely new to relationships, Linda had not yet determined if being apart was a common desire among couples. Kyle and Danny seemed to always be together. But she knew every couple was different; she knew, too, she would have to come to her own conclusions and decisions. It wasn't all up to Kirsten! Linda Sikorsky had a say in the matter; if she really wanted someone to share her house, to live with her in the quiet of the woods, she would have to press the matter at some point and prepare for whatever answers she got. She was tough. She would survive.

Abigail Creek had not survived, and Linda turned her thoughts to the unfortunate woman. It was not an accident, of that Linda was certain.

Abigail had fled, and Abigail had been pursued. A bicycle was no match for a speeding car rushing up behind it, and whoever had been chasing her had accomplished their mission. They had flung Abigail to her death and kept going. While she knew the family was the first place to look, they had all been at dinner. It would be impossible for any of them to slip away, drive back to CrossCreek Farm, frighten Abigail so terribly she raced out into the dark night on a bike, chase and run her down, and get back to the dinner table before anyone noticed. *Excuse me, I need to use the ladies' room and kill someone, be right back.* Or the men's room—there were Rusty Creek and Clarence to consider. But why kill Abigail in the first place? Why run someone down who was wearing only a nightgown and slippers, pedaling furiously and futilely on a rickety bicycle? It wasn't for something she owned or possessed; it was for something she *knew.* Abigail Creek was murdered for what had been inside her head, knowledge of something someone wanted kept secret forever. *Find the family's secrets,* Linda thought, finally beginning to slide from consciousness into sleep, *and there among them you'll find the killer.*

She heard the television volume rise slightly in the attic room as Kyle and Danny switched from talking to listening. She focused on the white noise coming from the small round machine on her nightstand, and she drifted away to dream of old women fleeing in the woods, fleeing from danger, fleeing from love, fleeing from all the harm that comes chasing from behind. She was a little girl on a bicycle in the dark, trying her hardest to escape the unknown as it barreled ever faster toward her on the road.

# CHAPTER NINE

Caroline Creek was exhausted. She had spent the day smiling at all the right times and at all the right people, the kind of fragile smile expected of someone whose mother-in-law had just died suddenly and horribly, the kind of smile people knew was forced but appreciated anyway and pitied. Poor Caroline, poor Clarence, poor Creek family. How could someone do something so cruel? At other times, too, she had shifted expertly into mourning mode, appearing on the verge of tears she held off with the dab of a Kleenex. She'd even excused herself a few times as neighbors dropped by uninvited and insisted on staying just until discomfort overtook them. Caroline needed a moment to gather herself; they understood completely.

She hadn't hated Abigail, that was too strong a word, but she was not devastated by her death and found the timing advantageous. She was not privy to the terms of the divorce between Clarence and Abigail Creek, now conveniently unnecessary, but she had worried for some time that her years living rent free in the CrossCreek Farm guest house with reliable but intellectually challenged Rusty Creek were coming to an end. Of course Abigail was satisfied with the terms of the divorce—whatever they were—she was getting half of everything, was she not? And the Farm was a big part of everything. Caroline doubted it could survive as half of its former self.

Abi had been complaining to her husband for years that Rusty and Caroline should be paying to live there. Clarence was a generous man, as evidenced by his secret embrace of his outcast daughter Justine. He might have agreed with his wife, had their son had a job. But Rusty had been spoiled. Justine had been spoiled, too, the children of wealth and a father who shared it too readily. Neither child had to work for what their father freely provided. It had not surprised Caroline, who came into the family when she and Rusty met as teenagers, that Justine's easy living and freedom from responsibility led to drugs and criminal behavior. It happened all the time with celebrities and the children of wealth. Clarence would take care of them. Clarence would give them money and shelter. Clarence would bail them out, whether from his daughter's brushes with the law or his son's gambling debts. Then came Charlotte Gaines, and a few years later a divorce nearing its final stage. What that stage included they would never know, but Caroline was sure it would not have been good for her and Rusty. For all her smiling and her sweetness and her, "It's okay, don't worry about me, I'll be fine" charade, Abigail Creek was an unforgiving woman. Just look at what she did to Justine, Caroline thought. Imagine what she had in mind for the rest of them.

"What are you doing out there?" Rusty called from the bedroom. He was in there with the TV on and the volume turned low, playing some game or other on his smartphone.

Caroline was grateful for the invention of word games and crazy birds, or whatever they were called; it temporarily relieved Rusty of his itch to gamble with real money. She didn't care if he spent hours every day playing with strangers across the virtual landscape, so long as he wasn't driving off to Atlantic City to squander the money his father gave him that month.

"Nothing, Sweetheart," she called back from the couch in the living room. She was sitting in the dark, smoking a cigarette. She'd quit two years ago, but given the circumstances and the stresses around them, she considered a few puffs at night a harmless indulgence. "I'll be along in a minute."

Caroline had once been in love with Russell Creek, or so she'd thought as a guileless sixteen-year-old. The pair met in science class at school. Rusty was the class clown, and what Caroline had seen as charmingly goofy she later realized was a certain dullness. He was quick to anger, and a juvenile anger at that, becoming offended at the slightest thing and acting like a child who'd had his toy taken from him. He let himself go, too, once they were married at twenty. He'd never been a jock, but he had been in very good shape in high school and Caroline foolishly thought he would work to maintain it. Instead he took for granted that she would always be with him, just like he took everything else in his life for granted. Twenty years and thirty pounds later he was still oblivious. He had no idea, for instance, that their way of life was in jeopardy ... or had been until last night. It had never occurred to him that his parents' divorce could affect them in any way, but Caroline knew. She suspected Clarence Creek was on the verge of selling CrossCreek Farm, giving half the proceeds to Abigail and leaving Caroline and Rusty to fend for themselves. She was just about to go to Abigail and plead when luck shined upon them on a dark New Jersey road. Nothing would have to be sold now, nothing would need to change.

She glanced at the bedroom as a slow exhale of smoke left her lips and doubt crept back into her mind. Was Rusty as clueless as she'd always thought? Had she underestimated his knowledge of their situation and, much more darkly, his ability to do something about it? He'd run several errands the last few weeks, explaining them vaguely—the drug store when nothing was needed, and that drive to the car wash she knew was closed that day for the owner's wedding. She had not confronted him about his movements, but now that Abigail had been murdered, she wondered ... and she shivered. There were worse things than being asked to leave the guest house, with prison high on the list.

Caroline had steered that meddling ex-detective and her New York friends away from Rusty and the farm. Justine was a more likely target than her ever-tipsy, petulant brother. And considering Abigail's fierce determination not to have Justine brought back into the family, to keep her exiled in every way, why not start with her? Abigail was furious to find out Clarence had kept in contact with his daughter all this time. When Abi could not have her way she made sure no one else did, either.

"Sweety?" Rusty called from the bedroom.

"Be right there!" Caroline said, crushing her cigarette out on the small plate she used as an ashtray. He would surely smell smoke on her, and he would not care. It had been a very trying day all around. Rusty had to stop playing his games while the family mourned and dealt with visitors. He could get back to them now, and she could smoke, it was a fair trade.

Caroline stood and closed her robe, pulling the belt tight. She left the dish with the cigarette butt on the end table, put the smile back on her face, and headed in to watch TV with the man of someone else's dreams.

# CHAPTER TEN

K yle and Linda were having coffee together on the back porch, watching the sun slowly blanket the landscape in spreading light as it rose through the trees. They'd independently had the idea of greeting the sunrise, and when Kyle came out on the porch he was not surprised to see Linda sitting at the metal table, staring out at the lawn. Sound traveled both ways in the small house; just as Linda had heard Kyle and Danny in the room above her, Kyle had heard Linda stirring several times during the night, walking into the kitchen, using the bathroom, going back to bed for another hour or two of fitful sleep. It was cold enough now for sweaters, and Kyle was wearing one Danny had given him the previous Christmas. It was almost a ritual: Danny gave Kyle a new sweater every year (with Kyle adding it to his growing collection and wondering where he would put them all), and Kyle giving Danny a fun pair of cufflinks. There were other gifts, of course, not to mention the stocking stuffers hung above the cardboard fireplace Kyle put out every year. Beside their stockings were one each for Smelly and Leonard, filled with cat toys, treats, and intoxicating brews of catnip. Linda was wearing an orange down jacket, more appropriate to the dead of winter than the cooling down of fall.

"May I join you?"

"I'd expect nothing less," Linda said, smiling at him as he sat across from her. "Danny coming?"

"Not yet. It's Sunday. He works the other six days, one way or the other. If he's not at the restaurant, he's on the phone with Chloe or a vendor or my mother."

"You think it was a mistake, getting your mother to invest in Margaret's Passion?"

Kyle thought about it a moment. Had his mother Sally not come through, they would have been in a much more difficult situation trying to come up with the money. This way they owned the restaurant, Margaret kept the building, and Kyle and Danny entered into a business venture with Sally Callahan.

"Yes and no," Kyle said. "It was a tradeoff. Immediate cash in exchange for going into business with family. She's getting better, she's letting up. Having a man in her life helps."

"How's that going?" asked Linda. Kyle's father died some years ago and Kyle was surprised when Sally told him last spring that she had met a man. At sixty-seven, Farley Carmichael was almost ten years younger than Sally and a widower himself. He had no children; what he did have was a successful boat business—yachts to be exact—that he'd grown into a major player in the luxury yacht world and sold for an undisclosed and very handsome sum. He owned a penthouse on Lake Shore Drive he had no intention of giving up or inviting Sally to occupy with him, which suited Kyle's mother just fine. She had blossomed the last few years in ways Kyle never anticipated; being an unmarried woman with a boyfriend and no plans of it ever being more was a role she enjoyed and adapted to easily.

"It's going fine as far as I know," Kyle said. "She's kind of a libertine, my mother."

Linda's brow shot up. Her own mother, though she had remarried after Peter Sikorsky's death, had not married a third time and would remain forever a double-widow, uninterested in meeting another man and certainly not in sleeping with one.

"They don't live together and probably never will. My mom discovered independence after my dad died. She was very happy with him, don't misunderstand me. But once she got past the grief she started discovering parts of herself she didn't know she had. She paints now, not great stuff, but it's not meant to be. She has friends in Chicago. And to be fair, I think she put marriage out of the picture as a way of respecting my father. She wants a man in her life. She doesn't want a husband."

Kyle saw Linda wince. He immediately regretted discussing his mother's independent lifestyle, knowing it echoed for Linda in her concerns about Kirsten.

"Maybe I was a fool," Linda said, looking away.

"Love is never foolish. It just has a way of taking the shape best suited to it. I'd been single for, what, fifteen years before I met Danny? I had no intention of giving up my apartment and everything in it and moving into a two-man, two-cat family. That's just the shape it took."

"And if he hadn't wanted to live with you?"

"Then it would have taken a different shape."

"Or faded away."

"I don't see that happening for you," Kyle said. "Kirsten loves you very much."

"She just doesn't love my house."

"You've only lived here for what, six weeks?"

"Let me finish!" Linda said, uncharacteristically sharp. "She doesn't love my house, or the thought of living together, or even of making plans beyond next week." She waved her engagement ring at him. "So what was this about? Is it a friendship ring? Call it that, then. Don't let me keep thinking next week, or the week after, or the month after that, she's going to suddenly get serious about our future together."

"Patience," Kyle said.

"I know, I know. It will take its own shape, and I have to decide if it's a shape that suits me."

They were silent then, watching as the sun broke over the trees surrounding Linda's property. It was truly rural, more woodsy than Kyle realized when they'd first arrived.

"It's so isolated here," he said. "You could drive along the road and not see another car for ten minutes.

"Or run someone down and be fairly certain you had time to disappear before anyone saw what you'd done."

"It wasn't one of them, it couldn't have been."

"Justine wasn't invited to the dinner. We don't know her whereabouts Friday night. I know you liked her, and I have a very nice painting now of my own front road, but it could be her."

"Or a hired gun."

"You mean a hired car," Linda said. "But first he was in the house with Abigail. Or she. Or them, for that matter, we might be looking at more than one person."

"Maybe it was someone who broke in thinking no one was there."

"But why chase her down and kill her?"

"Because she saw him."

Linda shook her head, thinking through possible scenarios. "We know it wasn't an accident. We know it was planned. Starting with the alarm on the house."

"Not quite," Kyle said. "It started with Abigail getting sick."

He was right. The whole reason Abigail Creek was alone in the house was because she'd gotten sick that afternoon.

"What would make someone ill but not kill them?" Linda asked. "It can't be food they shared, they would have all been sick."

"Maybe drugs of some kind, or a particularly nasty mushroom."

As murders go, this was quite different from the murders at either Pride Lodge or the Pride Gallery. This time there were multiple suspects and multiple motives, motives that would not be easily uncovered. Linda knew if they found one, they would find the other: if they knew why Abigail Creek had been killed, they would surely know who killed her.

Kyle started to say something and Linda quickly put her finger to her lips. "Shhh," she whispered, pointing out at the lawn.

Three deer and a fawn had crept out from the trees. They nibbled at the grass, their eyes darting everywhere while they ate, their ears pricked up as they listened and smelled for predators.

Kyle set his cup down and even that slight ping made the deer look up at the porch. Whether they saw Kyle and Linda or detected their scent on the wind, the deer went bounding back into the woods, followed instantly by the fawn.

"They're all over out here," Linda said. "They like my yard, it's sort of an all-you-can-eat lawn. Speaking of which ..."

Kyle waited. "Yes?"

"I think I need someone to help me with the property, the lawn, you know."

"Someone who helps a lot of your neighbors? Someone named Sly Mullen?"

"Exactly. What was it Justine said? 'It's the ones you don't notice who notice everything.' It might be very helpful to have a chat with Sly and see just what he's noticed lately."

"You're going to interrogate him at the wake?"

"I don't interrogate people anymore. I'm retired, remember? I might just ask him a few simple questions. People like to talk at these things, have a drink, let it out."

"While you'll be sticking with soda and listening to everything everyone says around you."

"As if you won't?" Linda said. She slid her chair back. "I'm about ready to start my day. You coming?"

"In a minute." He had almost started to talk about his photography, and his waning passion for it, when the deer leapt away. Passions change. The people in our lives change. Widowed mothers find boyfriends. Kyle had sensed for awhile now that changes were coming their way. Margaret Bowman was surely going to leave them soon, moving to Florida for her final years. His own boss, Imogene, would move on eventually to something better. He had Danny, that he knew. He had Detective Linda. He had the cats for a few more years. For some reason the inevitability of it all changing had been on his mind, and he reminded himself that it was time to set a date for their wedding and begin planning. That would not change and he wanted to be married at last before anything else could change. *You're being morbid, Kyle Callahan,* he thought. *Stop it. Life is as fleeting as those deer, but you don't need to worry. Everything is okay.*

"I'll see you in the house," Linda said. She knew Kyle was lost in thought and wanted to let him wander there undisturbed. She picked up her cup and headed inside.

Kyle looked up a moment after the back door closed and saw a deer peering at him from just beyond the tree line.

*Don't worry, little deer*, he thought, wondering if the creature could sense his thinking, smell his melancholy. *I won't hurt you.*

He heard Linda talking to Danny in the house and decided it was time to get moving, shake off the momentary blues and join life as it happened. One thing he was certain of, it wouldn't wait for any of them. Stay apace or fall behind and be left with reflections and what-ifs. The present only lasted for a moment before dashing away. He was determined to keep up with it. He waved at the deer in the trees and headed inside.

# CHAPTER ELEVEN

**R**ussell Creek was checking his email in the bathroom. It was the only place he felt he had complete privacy; it was also where he could experience panic, fear and, in the case of his mother's sudden and tragic death, relief, without exposing his emotions to his wife. Rusty was an open book, as Caroline had told him a thousand times. It's how she knew when he lied, when he behaved badly, and when he snuck around behind her back. "You skulk, Rusty," she would say. "Like a cat that's been caught in the catnip. Why are you skulking?"

The reason he'd been skulking lately was right there in his email: Carl Streeter, the local Hunterdon County loan shark, was reminding him that he owed Carl $10,000 and it was past time to pay up, with either cash or his knee caps. Rusty would have paid Carl already, had his mother not found the check from his father in the den and ripped it up, right in front of Rusty!

"It's over, Rusty," she'd said not two days ago, calling him on the carpet in the main house's living room. The one humiliation she had spared him was not having Caroline there to watch.

"I'll pay it back," he'd pleaded.

"Like you paid it back the last time, and the time before that?"

Rusty had stared at the tiny ripped pieces of check in her hand and nearly cried.

"What?" she said. "You thought the divorce would change things? That I'd just take a settlement and walk away, leaving you to leech off your father for the rest of your life? Oh, Russell, Russell, Russell. Things may be changing more than anyone knows."

He didn't know what to make of her statement, but he knew to take his mother at her word. She had thoroughly banished his sister Justine from the household, only recently discovering his father had renewed contact with her and was trying to bring her back into the family—soon to be a new family, with a new matriarch. He knew that was the real source of his mother's anger, no matter how hard she pretended otherwise. He felt like the victim of misplaced rage, and he didn't like it one bit.

Now he didn't have to dislike his mother's treatment of him. And while he had issues with her, he was very sorry she was dead. It was a terrible way to die, even for someone so vindictive. Still … it was convenient.

"Rusty? You in there?" Caroline said, knocking at the bathroom door.

*Well, of course I'm in here*, he thought. *Who the hell else would be in our bathroom?* "Yes, Sweety," he called back, sitting on the closed toilet lid. "Out in a sec, you know it takes me awhile sometimes in the morning."

He heard Caroline shuffle away from the door. He turned back to his iPhone, reading Carl's latest email. He had given Rusty another week to come up with the money, money that had been spent betting on horses that came in somewhere back of the pack, not first or second as Rusty gambled they would. Carl was out of patience; he was also no respecter of class or wealth, and more than one of his clients had vanished over the years, never to be seen or heard from again. Rusty assumed they were securely anchored to the bottom of the Delaware River.

He quickly typed an email back, saying he would have the money by mid-week. They just needed to get past his mother's funeral and he would ask his father for another check, this one left whole and cashed before the ink could dry.

Russell pocketed his phone and flushed the toilet for effect. He composed himself, hoping he would not be too transparent in his relief; he headed out of the bathroom, tempted to whistle a tune but restraining himself.

# CHAPTER TWELVE

Justine Creek could smell the odor of muffins, scones and coffee wafting up through the 150-year-old floorboards of her second floor apartment in Frenchtown. The house she lived in was almost as old as the small town itself. You could drive through Frenchtown in less than ten minutes, provided you kept to the speed limit. If you exceed it you'd make it in under five. Along the main road were restaurants, galleries, a bicycle shop, and Cup 'n Cake, the bakery and coffee shop that had moved into the store below Justine's apartment two years ago after the dress shop failed.

Justine was friends with Cathy, the perky young woman making a go of it downstairs. Cathy had a wife named Gladys. Both women were in their 30s and lived nearby in a rented house with four dogs and a cockatoo named Aristotle. They had kindly allowed Justine to put her paintings up for sale on the bakery's walls, and every now and then she even sold one.

It was a somber morning for Justine, but not one she'd call sad. She had loved her mother; she still did, on some level, or maybe it was just a kind of remembrance. Every child remembered times that were good, even if they had to be selective in their memories. On the day of her mother's wake she was not attending, Justine selected a few happy times she had shared with Abigail. Most were from her childhood, when her mother took her shopping, or showed her how to make lasagna while Justine watched beside her at the kitchen counter.

The good memories became harder to recall once Justine hit her teens. Her adolescence coincided with what she considered an emotional disturbance in her mother. Abigail Creek was bipolar; at least that's the diagnosis Justine later gave her, unsubstantiated by any doctor, since Abigail never saw one about her moods. Abigail would change dramatically, swinging from nice, concerned and engaged, to ecstatic, nearly manic; at other times she plunged into a darkness only she could see. And always the sternness, once the changes began, always the brittle attitude. Justine believed it was a fault not only of her father, but of the entire Creek family that no one dared broach the subject. They all pretended nothing was wrong. But Justine could not pretend. Justine became the recipient of Abigail's undefined, misdirected anger, and Justine began to deal with it as many teenagers dealt with problems they didn't understand and couldn't control.

It started with booze from her parents' extensive liquor cabinet, then moved on to pills she got from friends at school. Finally, when she was in high school, cocaine and heroin she sucked up her nose. She had never used a needle and was grateful for that small measure of good fortune: needles left many a user with hepatitis and HIV. Justine was healthy; she had escaped the worst.

The scars she was left with were not on her arms but in her heart. Abigail had kicked her out of the family when Justine was twenty-nine and she had kept that door slammed shut. Clarence did as he was told by his wife and shut out his daughter, too, but only for a few years. Then he heard that Justine had cleaned up her life, that she was clean and sober and painting. He tried to talk Abigail into reconsidering her position, but by then her own emotional problems had calcified into a stubborn hardness. She would not have Justine back in her house to steal another irreplaceable heirloom; never mind that Justine had not stolen anything in five years. And Abigail had set her sights on their son as well. He hadn't yet stolen anything she knew of, but given his gambling habit and his debts, his easy abuse of his father's generosity, Justine believed it was only a matter of time before Abigail banished him, too. She had been pressing for a year to have Clarence force Rusty and Caroline out of the guest house and into the real world. He had resisted, and now it didn't matter.

Justine knew these things from her clandestine phones calls, emails and occasional visits from her father. He would come into the farmers market when Abigail was off running errands or getting her hair done in Flemington. She loved her father dearly and wished she could be there to console him now. She knew he loved Abigail very much—or had at one time—and he might be the only one truly heartbroken over her loss.

She took another deep breath of the delicious smells rising up from the bakery and considered her options. Should she go to the funeral on Wednesday and watch from a distance? The only person who would protest would be in the casket. Or should she just send a wreath? What would happen now that there was no Abigail standing guard outside the family, keeping the black sheep out beyond the fence? And what would become of CrossCreek Farm itself? The last time she'd spoken to her father he seemed worried. Abigail was taking it all too well, he'd said. She seemed relieved with the divorce, almost gracious. He knew his wife's temper and wondered if there was something she hadn't told him. But what? What October surprise could she possibly have, and why not just be acrimonious? Unbeknownst to the others, Clarence was considering selling some of the land; he might not have any choice if half his assets were leaving with Abi. He didn't need a vineyard anymore, he told Justine. He was getting old and time had become more precious than success. But Abi ... Abi was up to something.

*She wants it all,* Justine thought at the time. *If she leaves you with half, she'll never believe she'd settled accounts in full. Abigail Creek does not do things halfway.* She had kept her thoughts to herself, but now she wondered if she had been right, and if she was not the only one to draw these conclusions. Abigail had been up to something, and someone had stopped her.

She took a sip of her jasmine tea and wished she'd said more to the retired detective when they came to see her. She didn't know anymore, really, but as she sat at her table imagining her mother's wake, she began to think things. She was sure the detective and her friend were thinking them, too. She hoped to see them again, at the market, or perhaps she would make a trip to the house on Lockatong Road. She could ask how the wake had gone, who had been there, and if anyone at all had cried.

# CHAPTER THIRTEEN

Had Kyle paid any attention to the weather report he would have known rain was coming. It started just after noon, moving in quickly and quietly with a cover of clouds that blanketed the Valley. It wasn't a hard rain, but a steady one, a step above drizzle that could chill the bone and turn a mood sour, which seemed to be the case with Danny and Kirsten. Neither of them wanted to attend the wake, wondering if it was improper for strangers to mingle with the mourners.

"We're not strangers," Linda said, driving to CrossCreek Farm along Route 651. "We found her, remember?"

"All the more reason it creeps me out," Kirsten said, staring out the passenger side window as the car cruised slowly along. She'd come over after breakfast and had made no appointments for today, Sunday. While she often worked the entire weekend, she knew things were getting to a critical stage with Linda and she wanted to be present. There were thing she needed to discuss.

"Listen," Kyle said, as determined as Linda to attend the wake and learn what they could, "there are likely to be a lot of people here. We can just mingle. Talk to some folks, have a drink if you need one to get through it, and leave."

"We won't stay long," Linda promised.

Danny stayed silent in the back seat next to Kyle. He'd had a phone call that morning from Chloe at the restaurant saying Margaret had fallen in her kitchen. It wasn't the first time, but Danny increasingly worried that the frail 82-year-old would take a tumble one of these days and break a hip. Broken hips for the elderly were often a push toward life's exit door. Losing her, to death or more likely to Florida, would be among the biggest challenges he knew were coming.

"How is she?" Kyle said quietly, knowing what occupied Danny's thoughts.

"She says she's fine. She didn't need a doctor or the hospital. But this is the second time in a month."

"It was wise having Chloe check on her every morning."

"Which means it was wise I made Chloe the day manager, despite your mother's interference."

"Wow," Linda said as she turned onto CrossCreek Road. Cars were parked all the way from the house to the main road, with some starting to double park, creating a single lane as they wound their way to the house.

"There won't be any parking closer," Kyle said, looking at all the cars.

"You're right. I'll just do what everyone else is doing and park … right here."

Linda eased to the right side, pulling up next to a large blue pickup. They parked, opened two umbrellas and headed slowly to the house, Linda and Kirsten huddled under one umbrella and Danny and Kyle under the other.

"A half hour tops," Kirsten said. "Please?"

"You got it," Linda replied. Kirsten had asked to stay the night, surprising Linda in the best way. She didn't want to ruin Kirsten's mood and upset their plans by staying too long at the wake.

Caroline Creek saw them coming up the driveway. She had been playing the part of hostess to a wake, among the most unusual and uncomfortable greeting duties anyone can have, and she was exhausted by the time the twentieth neighbor arrived. But it was also a part in which she she had no choice. Rusty certainly couldn't do it; he was socially awkward and already well into the booze by mid-afternoon. Charlotte, meanwhile, had not left Clarence's side for two days, not to mention she wasn't really family, not yet. It would have been improper to have her welcoming people to a wake for the woman she was replacing. Improper and, to many of Abigail's friends, unseemly. There were plenty who thought Abi was being overthrown, as so many women her age are, and the situation was tense enough just having Charlotte sitting next to Clarence on the couch or getting him another drink. They couldn't keep her out of sight, but they could keep her relatively quiet.

Opening the door as they arrived and closed their umbrellas, Caroline Creek smiled wearily and said, "Welcome, Detective. All of you, so glad you could come."

They could see from the front door how crowded the house was. They could hear it, too, as people from around the surrounding homes, from Stockton, possibly from as far away as Philadelphia, had all come to pay their respects. The noise was subdued—it wasn't a party, after all—but alcohol was being served and quite a few of the guests were helping themselves.

"May I take your coats?" Caroline said to Danny and Kirsten. They had both worn jackets, while Kyle was in a sweater and Linda had worn a dark navy pantsuit.

"I'll keep mine on," Kirsten said, hoping it would signal she didn't want to stay here long enough to get comfortable.

Danny handed her his jacket, which Caroline draped over her arm as she led them into the kitchen. "First stop is a drink," she said. "That includes coffee, water, tea, or something stronger. It's all set up, and all self-serve. I'll put your jacket, Mr.—"

"Durban," Danny said. "Danny Durban. But please, just Danny."

"Fine then, Danny. I'll put your jacket in the hall closet with the others. Help yourselves to anything you'd like. The main gathering is in the living room."

She ushered them into the kitchen and left. The kitchen didn't seem as large now that there were a dozen people standing in it, clustered in small familiar groups. The foursome knew none of them, and Kirsten immediately wished she'd stayed at Linda's house. She glanced at Danny: *Are you feeling as out of place as I am?* He understood the sentiment without saying a word, nodded, and met her at the large island counter that had been pressed into service as a bar. Neither of them was driving, so why not? Kirsten poured herself a glass of white wine, noticing the

CrossCreek Farm label, no surprise there, and Danny fixed himself a Vodka rocks.

Linda was a stranger to them all and wondered if coming had been a mistake. She and Kyle each got a cup of coffee from the large drip coffee maker by the stove, taking the chance for a quick huddle.

"We can't stay long," Linda said, her voice lowered. "We both might end up single if we do."

Kyle nodded. "Danny's not happy. But what's our objective, Detective?"

"I've been wondering about her sickness. It can't be a coincidence that Abigail got sick and stayed home."

"Agreed, but isn't that a conundrum? How would you get her to stay behind sick while the rest of them go to dinner?"

"By making her sick," Linda said, as if stating the obvious.

"Making her sick? But what if it killed her?"

"Maybe they were hedging their bets. They wanted her dead one way or the other. Maybe running her down was a backup plan. Or Plan C, more likely."

Kyle looked at her. "Plan C?"

"If whatever they did to make her ill didn't do the trick, then hire someone to break in, make it look like a burglary and kill the only witness. If that doesn't work—which it didn't—then seize the opportunity of Abigail fleeing on the bicycle and run her into the ditch."

"But there wasn't any burglary."

"Ah," Linda said, stirring creamer into her coffee. "There was no burglary because there wasn't time for one. She went running out of the house, quite possibly after seeing who was after her. They never staged a burglary because there wasn't time to."

"And they never set off the alarm because it wasn't on."

"Which they knew."

Linda turned and looked at the other people in the kitchen. She leaned back against the counter a moment, blowing on her coffee and speaking under her breath.

"Two things we need to know before we leave here: what exactly was wrong with Abigail Creek that kept her home Friday night, and who turned the alarm off, assuming Clarence turned it on, a possibly false assumption."

"You're forgetting a third," Kyle said. "We need to know who wanted her dead."

"That could be a multiple choice question."

Linda took a deep breath, cupped her coffee to steady it for a walk through the house, and headed into the living room. Kyle followed, with one quick glance back to Danny to let him know they wouldn't be here any longer than they needed to.

The living room was even more crowded than the kitchen. There must have been thirty people there, according to Linda's estimation. She recognized a few—Clara the muffin lady from the Farmers Market, and the exotic tea couple. It was a reminder to her how many neighbors she had not gotten to know in the short time she'd been living on Lockatong Road. It made her feel apart from them, the new kid on the block, which she was.

Clarence Creek was wearing the same clothes he'd had on the day before, although he'd shaved. His face was long and drawn, and he sat on the couch in almost the same spot he'd been on Saturday when they came to pay their respects. Charlotte Gaines had changed and looked fresh, wearing an eggshell blouse and long black skirt. She was wearing shoes today. She was not holding Clarence's hand this time and was standing behind him instead of sitting next to him.

Clarence glanced up when Linda and Kyle entered the room, offering a slight wave of his hand to acknowledge them, while Charlotte mouthed "Thank you," two words Linda assumed she'd been saying all afternoon. There was nowhere to sit—the folding chairs that had been put into the living room for visitors were all taken, as were the couches and overstuffed chairs—so Kyle positioned himself near the fireplace while Linda moved to the far side of the room by the piano.

Rusty Creek was sitting on the piano bench, its lid closed while he plucked imaginary notes on it. Within moments of standing near him Linda could tell he'd been hitting the bar long and hard; his head slumped, and when he glanced up at her his eyes were swimming in red.

"Who are you?" he asked, peering at her through an inebriated fog. "Oh wait, I remember. You were here yesterday. You're the ones who found her." He sucked in his breath, as if a sob might escape his throat.

"I'm very sorry," Linda said. "May I?" She slid onto the piano bench beside him.

"Why not, I can't play it. It would disturb the guests." There was a bitterness in his tone.

"Would you rather none of us be here?" she said.

"Of course! If none of you were here, it would mean my mother was still alive, wouldn't it?"

Linda felt foolish having asked the question.

"I wish she'd gone with us," Rusty said. "I kept telling her to come with us, it's just a stomach flu, you'll make it through dinner."

"Is that what was wrong with Abigail?"

Rusty reached for his glass of Vodka on the piano top. It was empty except for melted ice. He turned it up and drained it anyway.

"Stomach flu, virus, bug, whatever you call it."

"Had she eaten something that day? Were other people sick, too?"

"Just Mom, and no, no one else had it."

"What about the alarm?" Linda asked.

Rusty turned and stared at her. "What does that have to do with being sick?"

"Nothing, I'm just curious."

"How do you know we have an alarm?"

"I saw it by the back door, when your wife showed us the patio."

"Oh. So Caroline 'showed you the patio', did she?" Rusty would not be surprised if Caroline's meddling into his habits extended to telling everyone else about them. "Well Mother turned it off to go riding into the dark, didn't she?"

"I thought she might have been chased," Linda said carefully. "Given the nightgown, the slippers. I just wondered if anyone … if you saw any evidence of an intruder."

"I didn't, no. But then we had no reason to suspect one. She wasn't run down in the living room."

"The kitchen window was open," Caroline said, causing Linda to jump. Caroline had come up to the piano unnoticed. Linda wondered how much of their conversation she'd heard.

"But nothing else. Abi probably opened it for the breeze. She got hungry, she made herself something in the kitchen and she opened the window. This is her favorite time of year. *Was* her favorite time. Of course, she'd have to turn the alarm off to open the window. Mystery solved. As for turning it on, Clarence always does that when he leaves."

"Did you see him set it Friday night?" Linda asked.

"I wasn't paying attention."

"I came back in to piss," Rusty said. "Before the drive."

"And you turned it back on," Caroline said quickly. "I specifically remember asking you in the car. 'Did you turn the alarm back on, Rusty?' You said yes."

"I'm sure I did," said Rusty, not sure and not caring.

"Who else has the code?" Linda asked.

Caroline smiled, as if Linda Sikorsky were a dense child. "We all do!" She paused. "Including Justine, I'm quite sure."

There it was again, Linda thought. Pointing the finger at Justine Creek. Linda had already decided Justine was likely the last person to suspect in her mother's death.

Linda was feeling cornered now, with Rusty beside her on the piano bench and Caroline standing over her. "Excuse me," she said. "May I borrow your restroom?"

"Sure!" Rusty said too loudly. "Just be sure to give it back!" He let out a drunken cackle as Linda rose and headed in the direction Caroline pointed her.

"Down the hall," Caroline said. "It's a half bath. We have two full ones if it's occupied."

Linda nodded her thanks and walked away, leaving Rusty to glare and Caroline wondering what she was up to.

Kyle had been in the living room no more than five minutes when he realized he was completely out of place. He knew no one here, including the family. Their visit yesterday was all the contact he'd had with the Creeks, aside from standing beside Abigail Creek's body on the road while they waited for an ambulance to arrive. It was both an awkward situation and an opportunity—no one knew him, either, and he was not expected to interact with any of them. He could just lean on the wall by the fireplace, watch them all, and listen.

He noticed how proper Charlotte Gaines was being. She remained standing behind Clarence and only reached for his hand when his emotion threatened to bubble up again as people came over to shake his hand or occasionally hug him and offer words of condolence.

It was an odd arrangement that had him puzzled. He didn't spend time with any divorced couples but he was sure few of them included third players. He found it very unusual that Abigail Creek would not only spend time with Clarence and Charlotte, but that she would allow Charlotte to all but move into her home when the divorce had not yet been signed. Something about it made him think of the wolf welcoming the lamb to dinner … and now the wolf was gone. Perhaps the lamb had not been so fooled by the wolf's disguise.

The husband from the couple who'd sold Danny his tea at the Farmers Market walked over then, a red drink of some kind in his hand. "Cranberry juice," he said. "It's as strong as it gets for me." He placed it on the fireplace mantle and shook Kyle's hand. "Rupert. Rupert Kleven, your partner bought tea from my wife and me at the market."

"Yes, yes of course, I remember," Kyle said, shaking hands. "Amazing tea, we had some this morning. I can taste the peach so clearly."

"I suppose that's why they call it Peachtree." Rupert took up a place next to Kyle and looked around the room. "Tragic about Abigail."

"Tragic."

"We knew her from the market. Her and Clarence, and the daughter Justine. Can't say I know anyone else here except from sight."

"Well, that's about fifty more than I know!"

The two men surveyed the room, watching people interact in subdued tones, forming cliques as people often do in large gatherings.

"Have you known the family long?" Kyle asked.

"Just as long as we've had a booth at the market, six months or so. Abigail came in from time to time. I never saw her talk to her daughter, though. They avoided each other, even in the same room."

Kyle wasn't surprised. Neither woman seemed the type to cede ground to the other.

"Clarence was fond of our cinnamon rooibos chai. That's how I remember people, by the teas they buy. You?"

"I'm not that adventurous, and I mostly drink coffee."

"No, I don't mean your favorite tea. How you remember people."

"Ah," said Kyle. He thought about it a moment. "I'm a photographer."

"Really?"

"Not, you know, professionally, although I had a show in Manhattan last spring. But it's my pastime, and that's how I remember people. I take pictures of them, or imagine taking pictures of them, and then …" He hesitated, feeling silly telling this to a stranger. "I caption them."

"You caption them?"

"Yes." Kyle turned and looked squarely at him. "'Still life with Rupert and tea leaves. Something like that. Lame, but it works."

Rupert smiled. Then, nodding toward Clarence and Charlotte, he said, "How would you caption them?"

"That's what I'm trying to decide."

"It's an unorthodox family, that's for sure. The last time I spoke with Clarence was maybe a month ago, he came in looking for a soothing tea."

"Nerves?" Kyle asked, not surprised that a man in the middle of a divorce might need a sedative.

"Not at all. Soothing to the stomach. He was taking medication for a heart arrhythmia and it was giving him cramps. He said he'd rather take tea for his condition but I told him there are some things even tea can't help. That was the last time I spoke to him until today. Very sad."

Neither man had much else to say, both having come out of some sense of obligation, and both wanting to leave as soon as possible. Kyle looked around the room again, thinking of an exit strategy, when he realized someone was conspicuously absent. He hadn't seen him in the kitchen, and he wasn't in the living room.

"Say, have you seen Sly Mullen here?"

"Sly who?" said Rupert, and Kyle realized there was no reason for the tea seller to know who he was talking about. "Tell me what kind of tea he drinks and I might remember."

"Never mind. He's the gardener. Landscaper. I'm not really sure exactly what he does, but he does it for a lot of these folks. I was expecting to see him here."

Rupert picked up his glass of cranberry juice from the fireplace mantle, looked across the room and caught his wife's eye. He discreetly held up his watch: time to go. "You take care, Kyle."

"Peachtree."

"Yeah," Rupert said, laughing lightly. "Mr. Kyle Peachtree. And if you're in the neighborhood again, stop by. Try some chicory next time." He winked at Kyle and headed across the room.

Kyle looked around again. Sly was definitely not there. For someone who was described as a reluctant member of most of the families represented here, his absence seemed peculiar. Kyle wandered away, looking for Linda to tell her the man who noticed everything was noticeably not there. He also wanted to tell her about Clarence looking for a soothing tea. It seemed stomach trouble ran in the family. When he looked toward the piano at the far end of the room he saw she was gone. Only Rusty remained, his head bowed as he stared blankly at the covered piano keyboard. Caroline was standing next to him, leaning down and whispering. Kyle decided to wander the house and see if he could find the good detective.

Linda had excused herself as a way out; she'd felt trapped between Caroline and Rusty Creek and needed room to breathe. A bathroom was as good a place as any to gather her thoughts, focus, and decide what to make of the new information she had.

The alarm was off. The kitchen window was open. Abigail had stayed behind, feeling ill most of the day. Rusty had gone back inside to use the bathroom, but said—or was told by Caroline to say—he had turned it back on. None of it was coincidental; while coincidence was a common occurrence in every day life, it had no place in a murder as planned out as this had been. Pieces had to fall into place, or be put there. Beginning with an illness. But what would reliably make someone ill?

Not expecting to find anything, but thinking it might stir her imagination, Linda opened the medicine cabinet and looked to see what secrets it revealed. A lot can be learned from the prescription bottles, toiletries and other odds and ends people put in their bathroom cabinets. A man's razor in a woman's apartment, or eyebrow curlers in a man's. She hadn't expected to find much in a half-bath, but on the other hand …

Band-Aids, Q-Tips, aspirin, tampons, the usual things, but then she saw a pill bottle, turned with its label facing away. She took it out and read the label: Quinidine. *What the hell is Quinidine*, she wondered, as she read the instructions beneath Clarence Creek's name. It said to take one pill three to four times a day. *Quinidine … Quinidine …* Then it hit her: her aunt Celeste, who'd died from a heart attack on her back porch, had been taking this medication for several years. It was used for an irregular heartbeat. But what were its side effects? What would it do if you gave it to someone who didn't know they were taking it? She made a mental note to look into the drug and put the bottle back just as a knock came at the door.

"Are you alright in there?" It was Caroline's voice, followed by another light knock.

Linda quickly ran water in the sink to cover the sound of the cabinet closing. She took a deep breath, turned and opened the door.

There stood Caroline, with Kyle looking over her shoulder.

"Your friend Kyle's been looking for you," Caroline said.

Linda hoped they didn't notice her blushing. "I'm fine, fine, I just … needed a moment. Finding Abigail on the road like that, coming to the wake …"

"And you a virtual stranger." She was no longer offering a practiced smile.

"You're right," Kyle said, stepping in as he realized something was up with Linda. "We really should be going."

"Yes," Caroline said, glancing past Linda into the bathroom. "I mean, it's difficult enough for those who knew Abi. I can't imagine having found her on the road like that."

Caroline ushered Linda and Kyle back into the living room. "We really appreciate your coming, I knew it wasn't something you had to do. Let me get Danny's coat." She left them standing near the kitchen entrance where Kirsten and Danny were waiting, anxious to leave.

Linda glanced into the kitchen and saw it had emptied out in the short time they'd been there. Many of the people had come, like them, to pay respects and head back out to their days. Grief was as uncomfortable when it was someone else's as it was when it was your own. What do you say to someone who has just lost a loved one? "I'm sorry for your loss," is something Linda had said many times in her job investigating deaths. They were words spoken when death was sudden and inexplicable, and more often when a life had simply come to its natural end.

Caroline returned with Danny's jacket and handed it to him. She had tired of their presence. She led them to the front door, managing a last smile as she opened it on the still falling rain.

Linda stopped a moment in the doorway. "Oh, does Clarence have a heart condition?"

"What an odd question," Caroline replied, staring at her. "Yes, yes he does. Are you a doctor, too?"

Linda's question startled Kyle. He was going to mention what he'd learned when they were back in the car.

"Just curious," Linda said.

"Many a cat has died from curiosity."

Linda thought of Abigail. What had she been curious about? Had she satisfied her curiosity at the price of her life?

"I'm sorry for your loss." It was all Linda could think to say.

The four of them hurried out to the car, the sound of the rain broken only by the firm closing of the door behind them. Linda knew if they came back it would be under very different circumstances, and they would not be welcome.

# CHAPTER FOURTEEN

Charlotte stared into the medicine cabinet, thinking something wasn't right. She could swear she'd left the pill bottle on the second shelf and now it was on the bottom. It was her job to make sure Clarence took his heart medication three times a day. She kept it in the half-bath because he didn't like taking it, didn't like admitting he had to take it, and never wanted the reminder of seeing the bottle in his own bathroom. Could she have put it back on the wrong shelf? No, she didn't think that was possible. The only answer was that someone had moved it. But why would anyone move a pill bottle? And who? There had been upwards of fifty people in the house that day, any one of them could have come in here. She knew people often went through the medicine cabinets of other people's homes looking for something to abuse. But heart medication? Of course, they wouldn't know what it was. And if they'd stolen any pills and took them, well, good luck, she thought. That's not a trip you'll enjoy.

So many things had fallen into place the last month that Charlotte believed it was meant to be: Abigail taking the low road in the divorce, demanding it all instead of wisely walking away with half and being happy to have it. Clarence discovering a heart problem—not something Charlotte wanted, but another stroke of fortune. She knew luck was neither good nor bad, it was just luck. He had to take something for his condition, and that something came in the small pills in the bottle she was looking at. She had been formulating a plan for weeks and had run through several scenarios in her mind, none of them working out flawlessly as they needed to. Then the illness, and the Quinidine, and the side effects, and she had what she needed.

"What's wrong?" Rusty asked behind her, causing her to jump as she closed the medicine cabinet and saw him in the mirror. She wondered how long he had been standing there, watching her.

"Nothing, Rusty. I was just cleaning up in here."

"I didn't tell her he had a heart problem."

"Who's that?" she said, walking past him. He followed her down the hallway.

"The cop lady. She was very curious. She thought I was drunk."

"Weren't you?"

Charlotte had never cared much for Rusty. He was a slippery one, always moving around like a cat—a fat, inebriated cat—showing up in bathroom mirrors and listening behind doors.

"I'm on your side," Rusty said, as they entered the empty living room and Charlotte began picking up the debris of the wake. Their house-keeper Eloise had been there that afternoon but she'd come as a mourner and would not be back until Thursday.

"I don't know what you're talking about, Rusty, and I'd rather not. Where's Caroline?"

"Probably going through the books while Dad takes a nap. We won't be losing half the farm now … at least not to Mother."

He made Charlotte's skin crawl.

"You know, Charlotte," he said, picking up a half-full glass someone left on the coffee table. He held it up to the light as if that would tell him its contents, then he shrugged and drank it down. "I think an angel might have smiled on us. Don't get me wrong …"

"I never do."

"Mother's death is terrible, especially the way it happened, but we can't bring her back, and the fact is it changes everything by changing nothing. You understand?"

"No, I don't, and I don't want to. If you're not going to help me clean up this place then let me get to it in silence."

"Fine." He handed her his empty glass. "People think I'm stupid. I know that. They think I can't really do much but gamble and drink. They're right about the bets and the booze, but very wrong about the stupid. Good night, Charlotte."

He left her then, turning and walking out of the room. When he was almost into the hallway he stopped and turned back. "I came back in to use the bathroom."

"What are you talking about?"

"Friday night. Remember? We were in the car and I came back in to piss before the drive."

"I seem to remember," she said, feeling the chill in his voice.

"I went to turn the alarm off—it takes me more than sixty seconds to urinate—and it was the strangest thing … it wasn't on."

"Your father must have forgotten."

"He never forgets." Rusty turned away and walked down the hallway. Just before he was out of earshot, he said behind him, "I left it off."

Charlotte stood in the room, Rusty's twice-used glass in her hand. She felt like throwing it at him. He was as cunning as he was dull. What was that saying? You don't kill a snake by cutting off its tail. Rusty might be in need of a little decapitation. Charlotte would have to wait and see where he took this. If he had any sense—which he didn't—he would steer clear of her.

She went back to picking up glasses and paper plates. She thought about the "lady cop" as Rusty had called her. She thought about Rusty himself, and Caroline. She would need to make a trip to Stockton in the morning, for supplies and a private conversation. She was suddenly glad of the empty house, the silence. She needed them to think clearly and quickly. *Live in the solution*, she told herself, *not the problem*. She'd read that in a magazine or heard it on television, probably from some reformed addict. They were great at platitudes. Sometimes they were even right.

Charlotte Gaines met Abigail Creek at a cooking class five years ago. Young Mother Hubbard's was a restaurant in Lambertville, since gone out of business but thriving at the time. Its owner and head chef, Lillian Hubbard, grew up in the area and thought it was the perfect place to launch her culinary career. While the restaurant did not prove successful in the long haul, Lillian's career flourished and she moved to San Francisco when the business failed. But at the time things were going well and she taught cooking classes on Monday nights when the restaurant was closed. It was only a half hour drive for Charlotte from Trenton, half that for Abigail. Both women had been on a cooking craze, and it proved to be just one of the many things they found they had in common.

Charlotte was twenty years younger than Abigail, but not so young that the age difference was a problem. Charlotte was closing in on forty at the time, Abigail just about to turn fifty-nine. Not so far apart at all.

The class only ran for three weeks, and Charlotte often thought that had they not been paired together to work on the cream puffs everything would have turned out differently. They would not have bonded; they would not have gotten to know each other as well and as easily as they did. Abigail would never have told Charlotte about her family and her family's wine business, or introduced her to Clarence; and Charlotte would never have revealed her life in so many details to this new friend, just about every detail but one. Charlotte had a child when she was only fourteen, the result of a rape by her uncle. Sonny Gaines was now twenty-five. It was easy enough to do the math and realize how young she had been. When she told her parents about it they treated her like an overly-sexed teenager and her mother demanded she tell no one her uncle was the child's father. Charlotte kept her mouth shut; she kept the baby, too. That was the deal she'd made with the devil. Sonny Gaines was her great secret, her painful, hidden embarrassment. Some people also believed he was the reason Charlotte's uncle disappeared fifteen years later, having gone for a drive and never returned. His truck had been found abandoned on one of the many country roads in the area, but his body never would be.

Except for the fact she was the mother of an adult child, Charlotte shared everything with Abigail. It never occurred to Abi they would share her husband, too. That came later, as the marriage began to falter. There was friction over Clarence's infidelity—with his daughter Justine. Abigail was furious to know the two were in contact and when Clarence refused to banish Justine back to oblivion, she complained bitterly to Charlotte. She complained also of her no-account son and his leeching wife, living rent free in the guest house. There wasn't much Abigail did not complain about, and when Clarence first looked at Charlotte with more than a friendly gaze, Charlotte understood why he would have needs. Poor Clarence, she'd thought. Harassed, denied, sometimes even belittled by the woman he had been with since high school. A successful man like that deserved better, and Charlotte decided three years into her friendship with the family that she was just the person to provide it.

Clarence was asleep on his side while Charlotte lay in bed beside him, thinking things through. It had been such a long day. She wasn't given much to guilt. She decided at the tender age of fourteen that guilt was for the guilty, and she had done nothing wrong. She had become a mother against her will. She had struggled to survive when her parents divorced two years later and neither one wanted her and her bastard child. She had been on her own since then, just Charlotte and Sonny making their way in a brutal world. Whatever she did, she did to survive, and there was no guilt in that.

Oh, Abi, she thought, staring in the dark at the ceiling. I really did like you. Things seemed to be going along well, but then you had to have a secret of your own. If you had just kept it to yourself everything would have been fine. Secrets are such deadly things, she thought, rolling on her side to try and sleep. The ones we keep can eat us alive.

She knew it could be hours before she finally slept, if she did at all. She closed her eyes. Some people counted sheep when they needed to drift away. Charlotte counted country roads, until she finally got to the one with the abandoned truck, an empty driver's seat where her uncle had been. It always gave her comfort and she felt herself sliding off the shore of wakefulness, into the foam of dreams.

# CHAPTER FIFTEEN

It was an exhausting day for everyone. By the time they left CrossCreek Farm, Linda knew the best thing they could do was go back to the house and relax—no more talk of murder, suspects or motives, at least not with Kirsten there. She would wait until the morning when Kirsten headed off to work and then reconvene with Kyle. He'd sensed it too, the growing weariness of Danny and Kirsten to be caught up in this chase. Linda and Kyle decided to leave it alone for the rest of the day. Nothing more could be done on a rainy Sunday, so why not just enjoy themselves, eat a home cooked meal and get to know each other a little more. The men's vacation was quickly passing; there was no need to give a killer more of their time today.

Kirsten surprised them by making dinner. In the ten months the women had been together, Linda knew Kirsten to cook only two or three times. Linda was curious when Kirsten asked them to stop at the grocery store on the way home. Was something up? Was this some kind of special meal? Kirsten had made one of those the night she proposed to Linda. Come to think of it, each time she had cooked she had used it as a preface to something she wanted to say: the first cooked meal had gotten their relationship from acquaintances to dating. Another had put an engagement ring on Linda's finger. Was this one to remove it? Was it to prepare Linda for bad news, good news, or no news at all? Linda kept waiting throughout the meal for some indication of what would follow it. Almond encrusted tilapia, roasted Brussels sprouts, a beet salad with figs and goat cheese. If an announcement was coming, it would be a big one. The more they delighted in the food, the more worried Linda became that dessert would be a breakup. But nothing was ever said;

the meal was delightful from start to finish, and when it ended Kirsten insisted on clearing the table and putting the dishes in the dishwasher herself. That, Linda knew, was unprecedented, and as she sat in the living room with Kyle and Danny finishing their glasses of wine, she knew a conversation was coming.

"You okay?" Kyle asked. He and Linda were on the couch while Danny eased back in the recliner Linda had seen her aunt in so many times.

Linda looked at him and gently shook her head to say: let's not talk about this, I'm fine, I'll tell you in the morning.

They heard Kirsten finishing up. Danny rose from the recliner and said, "Kyle, let's go upstairs. Your mother's sent me some drawings for the renovation."

"Renovation?" Linda said. "You're renovating Margaret's Passion?"

Sally Callahan had been pressuring Danny since they bought the restaurant to modernize it. She respected Margaret Bowman, but she thought the décor was very outdated. Danny knew that was one of the things that attracted people to the place, the comfort of it, the quiet and slightly ragged elegance.

"No," he said, "we're not. But I have to indulge Sally."

"Never do business with family or friends," Kyle said, setting his glass on the coffee table and standing. He knew this was not about the drawings, but about leaving the two women alone downstairs.

"What's done is done. I've learned a great deal about how to deal with her. She just wants to be listened to, that's all. So I listen."

Kirsten came back from the kitchen drying her hands on a small towel.

"We're heading upstairs," Danny said. "The dinner was amazing."

"I have to keep in practice," Kirsten said, winking. "Besides, Linda's better at murder investigations than soufflés."

The men bid them goodnight and headed upstairs. Kyle let the wooden door down behind them, shutting them apart. The door was meant to keep heat in the bottom of the house, but it served perfectly as a divider, giving the women the privacy they needed.

Kirsten said nothing of greater significance as she and Linda finished up what little clearing there was to do. Linda washed the men's wine glasses by hand, the stems making them too delicate for a dishwasher. She kept waiting for any indication that Kirsten wanted to have a heart to heart with her, but none came. The quieter Linda was, the more Kirsten hummed and smiled. *She's enjoying this,* Linda thought. *I know this woman can be many things ... but cruel? I had no idea.*

Finally Kirsten set the dishtowel down and left the kitchen. Linda followed, expecting them to head into the bedroom for the night, but instead Kirsten veered into the bathroom. Linda kept walking and Kirsten stopped her.

"Where are you going?" Kirsten said, standing by the bathtub.

Linda returned to the doorway and stood there, watching Kirsten pull back the shower curtain.

"I thought ..."

"You thought wrong," Kirsten said. She leaned over the tub and turned the water on to fill it. "You do that a lot, my love."

*My love?* Linda was confused now. This was not a term to be used with someone you were about to discard. Linda carefully walked into the bathroom.

"I didn't just buy food at the grocery," Kirsten said. She stood up from the tub and held out a small green bottle. "Bubble bath!"

Flabbergasted, Linda stammered, "Bubble bath? But we never ..."

"Then it's time we should." Kirsten opened the bottle and let a stream of liquid fall into the hot water filling the bathtub. She capped the bottle, walked to Linda and closed the door behind them. "Don't scream this time," she said playfully. "You're a screamer, Detective, and we have company."

Linda's worries left her then, melting away in the steam rising from the bathtub. Whatever Kirsten had in mind, breaking Linda's heart was not it.

An hour later the women were in bed, listening to music playing from Kirsten's iPod on speakers she'd brought from home. Linda had never been much into music. She would listen on someone else's radio, and her mother in Philadelphia always had some classical station on. Linda preferred silence, especially at night. Her thoughts did not like the competition. But she wasn't alone tonight, and she was more than happy to listen to whatever Kirsten had on her playlist.

"You know," Kirsten said, her hands folded below her breasts as she lay on her back looking up at the ceiling, "it's not so bad out here in the woods. I've always been a city girl, if you can call New Hope the city."

"To some people it is. My aunt Celeste thought New Hope was very fast-paced. She'd been out here in the woods so long. I wish you'd met her."

"I wish you'd introduced me."

It stung, but Linda knew it was not deliberate. She regretted never bringing Kirsten to the house when Celeste was alive. Coming out of the closet was quick in some respects, very slow in others. Celeste knew Linda was gay, and had not been the least surprised, but Linda wasn't ready to introduce her aunt to her girlfriend. It was always going to be next week, then the next week, and finally it would never happen because Celeste was dead. One week after the funeral Linda took Kirsten to Philadelphia to meet her mother Estelle. She was determined not to have another regret.

"Listen," Kirsten said carefully. "I know you've been worried ..."

"Not at all."

"Don't say that. I know you have, and I can understand it. But everything is fine, Linda. We're fine. This is it for me, and I couldn't be any more truthful, sincere or convinced of that."

Linda's heart filled at the words. She felt her fears lessening by the moment, falling away after growing steadily for the last two months.

"It's been awhile for me," Kirsten continued. "The last relationship I was in ... it ended badly, we're not friends, and I'm just careful, that's all."

"I thought you were changing your mind. I thought you were set in your ways and here I was moving out to the country, and that was the end of that."

"I like it here. I just have to get used to the idea of living in the woods. I mean, really, Linda, 'the sticks' is an understatement."

"I could sell it, move to New Hope with you."

"No. This was your aunt's house, you love it here. And that's exactly the kind of thing that plants resentments that can erode a marriage for years until it finally crumbles from the inside."

There it was, that word. *Marriage.* Linda slowly twisted the engagement ring on her finger. Just a few hours ago she was afraid she'd be asked to take it off.

"I think it would be better for me to sell my condo," Kirsten said. "When the time comes."

After a moment, Linda said, "When might the time come?"

"To sell my condo?"

"To get married."

"Well, maybe your friends Kyle and Danny might be interested in a double ceremony."

"Are you serious?" Linda rolled on her side, facing Kirsten. "They're talking about the spring, that's not far away. And shouldn't they be your friends, too? I mean, a double wedding is kind of intimate."

"I was joking. Sort of. But the timing sounds about right."

"Where is all this coming from?" It seemed like a sudden turnaround, unless she was so bad at reading signals she had gotten everything terribly wrong.

"It's coming from my heart, Linda. And you're right, I don't know them well enough. A wedding is a special day, forget I suggested that, even if I was half-joking. But sometime next year."

"You really mean that?"

"I really mean it."

Linda wondered if something had happened to change Kirsten's mind. Seeing all those gay people happy with themselves at Pride Lodge had been such a moment for her, making her finally want to embrace who she was. Had Kirsten had a moment of clarity, something that made her think it was now or never? Linda was tempted to ask but left it alone; the evening was too special to risk prying into Kirsten's motives.

"Being set in my ways has cost me more than once," Kirsten said. "A life without you is not a price I'm willing to pay. Now tell me what song we're listening to. Consider it a final test of your intentions."

Linda smiled. Kirsten was being playful now, something Linda hadn't seen for awhile. She listened to the music coming out of the speakers on the dresser across from them. She recognized the man's voice, scratchy and very distinctive. She knew it was a famous song. She listened a moment more, and when she heard the lyrics, "*But we're along now and I'm singing …*"

"'A Song for You,'" she blurted. "Leon somebody."

"Leon Russell. One of the most beautiful songs ever written, and no matter who's singing it, it's for you, that one special person in your life. We're alone now, Linda …" She turned on her side to face Linda, then pulled herself close, easing in for a kiss. "And this song's for you."

The women embraced. Linda breathed in the smell of Kirsten's hair, the scent of the bubble bath that remained on them both. All was suddenly well in Linda Sikorsky's world.

She heard the intruder while she was still dreaming. Linda had long slept in launch mode, ready to answer her phone in the middle of the night when a body had been found, or to become instantly alert if someone came into her home uninvited.

She rolled over quickly and quietly, reaching for the gun in her nightstand. It was her father's gun, a Colt .45 Series 70 government model. He had used it when he was Military Police in Vietnam and kept it with him on the Cincinnati Police Force. He had not had it with him when a robber's bullet struck him outside the grocery store that fateful day. He'd had no reason to carry it on a mission to buy milk and cereal. Linda's favorite cereal. They'd run out and she wanted it for breakfast. Rather than tell her to eat what they had at home, he'd gone to the store. It was something Linda had blamed herself for from the age of eight, and no matter how many times (certainly in the thousands) she told herself it was not her fault, and her mother told her it was not her fault, she had lived with the guilt for thirty-five years. Her mother gave her the gun when Linda joined the New Hope Police, but she did not use it on the Force. It was too precious and Linda had kept it at home all these years.

She could hear Kirsten snoring lightly as she listened for the next sound. It was not Kyle and Danny. She knew the distinctive sounds of each man, and neither had come down the stairs. There was someone in the house. She slid smoothly out of bed, the gun in her hand. She crept toward the bedroom door, then heard it again, but this time it was a door—the back door that led into the garage. Linda had fallen into the habit of leaving it unlocked when the garage door was down. Someone who came in that way would have to get into the garage first. For some reason she hadn't considered that anyone ever would! It was one of those things about country living she had to get used to: just because you think no one's out here in the pitch black night doesn't mean you're alone. She opened the bedroom door carefully and clearly heard someone fleeing down the driveway. It was a pursuit now. Linda hurried through the kitchen, into the back room her aunt had used for crafting and storage. She saw the back door open and stopped. Might he have an accomplice waiting for her? Had she been tricked? But no, she heard a car start on the road and knew that somehow the intruder had been frightened off. Maybe he'd known she was coming—bad people had instincts, too. She rushed into the garage and saw the door open halfway. She knew it had been down and locked and made a mental note to have it fixed. If someone could open it that easily, she would never sleep well again here.

She ducked under the garage door and out onto the driveway just as she saw a car pulling away on the road. She ran and stood at the entrance to her drive, staring down Lockatong Road as the car's tail-lights reached Route 651 and turned left. She wondered if it was the same car Abigail Creek heard coming up behind her just before it ran her down.

She let the .45 drop slowly to her side. She almost regretted not having a chance to use it. She kept it cleaned, loaded and ready, and had fired it many times at the range. Her father had not had it with him when he needed it most, but Linda had. She turned and walked back into the garage, wondering if she should keep this to herself or tell the others in the morning. She decided it would only frighten them, and possibly make Kirsten think twice about living here. She knew sleep would not come again, so instead of returning to bed she put the gun in the coat closet and made herself a cup of coffee. The sun would be coming up in an hour or two and there was much to do. She would be the intruder next time, and she would arrive without a sound.

# CHAPTER SIXTEEN

Sonny Gaines was not scared of anything or anyone, and he would be the first to say it. You don't get through the kind of hardscrabble life he'd lived without being fearless. He certainly wasn't afraid of ghosts—he didn't even believe in the stupid things—so what had spooked him in that room off the garage? He'd slipped the garage lock easily enough, just slid his knife blade in and pulled. These back road country bumpkins didn't have enough sense to get good locks or use alarms. He supposed they thought no one would be coming along at four in the morning unless they were delivering newspapers, and who the hell did that anymore? But he had pulled the garage door slowly up, just enough to slip under, and the back door was unlocked! Easy peasy, nothing to it. He'd crept into the house, barefoot this time. His shoes were in the car; he had learned from his mistake at CrossCreek Farm. He wasn't sure if being shoeless made a difference, but when he listened for the sound of his own footsteps he heard nothing, so it must help. He'd climbed the few short steps up into the house, waited a long moment for his eyes to adjust to the darkness—and then he'd seen her. *Who the fuck are you?* There in the doorway leading into the kitchen. *What are you doing out here? It's the middle of the fucking night!* An old woman just standing in the doorframe staring at him, like she was going to stop him. He moved forward, gripping the knife he'd used to open the garage door. *You wanna die tonight, is that it?* Then she opened her mouth and he heard it—the highest, harshest scream he had ever heard in his life. He clapped his hands over his ears, nearly stabbing himself with the knife blade. He turned and ran out the back, under the garage door and out to the road.

His mother hadn't told him there was an old woman in the house, damn her. She was just an old woman, too, not a ghost. *So why could you see through her?* He shrugged it off, chalked it up to nerves, as he drove back to Trenton. Following the speed limit, being careful not to be pulled over for any reason. The last thing he needed was a record of any kind that he'd been on the road tonight.

He'd broken into the house without a plan. He wasn't good at planning. He only meant to frighten the people there, let them know someone was watching them, someone dangerous. But then the old woman was there, staring at him. And that scream! That's what spooked him, made the hair on his arms stand up and sent a chill down his spine. It wasn't the old bitch from the farm, he'd seen her well enough in his headlights to know what she looked like. It couldn't be her anyway, he told himself. There were no such things as ghosts. So what the hell was the old woman in the doorway? He hadn't stayed to find out; he'd turned tail and run.

He blushed at the thought of running. Sonny Gaines was no coward. He should have stayed and finished the job. But no, he had fled in terror. Like a boy. Like a boy who had taken orders from his mother all his life and was now on the edge of some very deep, deep shit because of it. Fuck his mother. She was going to have to do her own dirty work, and soon. Sonny had no intention of getting himself killed and ending up some ghost in a doorway. *She wasn't a ghost. You imagined her. You're slipping, Sonny, it's the nerves, you gotta settle the nerves.*

He made it back to his machine shop just before five o'clock. The sun was seeping light into the sky as he pulled his Mustang around back, parking it on the grass behind the trailer that doubled as an office and his home. Time for a drink. Beer was his favorite, but he might have to hit the whiskey tonight.

Sonny Gaines was as reluctant to be seen with his mother as she was to be seen with him. Their age difference wasn't much, and by the time he was a teenager people assumed she was his older sister. What made it so much worse was her shame, as if she was embarrassed to be seen with him, let alone claim him as her son. There was the blame, too. Sonny knew she blamed him for existing. She blamed him for the rape by her uncle. She blamed him for every shitty thing that had ever happened to her. Oh, she never said it outright, she didn't have to. It was the way she kept him hidden, and the fury he saw firsthand. There are many ways to punish a child; one was to hurt them, another was to own them. His mother had owned him from the day he was born, and he hated her for it. He hated her in the particularly dark way that finds its expression in loyalty and professions of love. Sonny knew "I love you" meant "I hate you" for a lot of people. It was the way they kept their damaged hearts a secret. Sonny was a battered soul, but he would not admit it, not even to himself. Instead he promised himself he would leave soon and never look back. He would not tell Charlotte where he went, nor would she ever hear from him on Mother's Day or Christmas. Hers might even be the last throat he cut.

*Sonny, Sonny, Sonny*, he heard his mother's voice say in his head as he drank straight from a pint of Jack Daniel's. *You never cut anyone's throat, you never broke anyone's legs. All you did was run down a helpless old woman on a bicycle, and I commend you for that. But really, Sonny, get a grip. You're just a boy who wants to be a man and never will.*

Don't forget your uncle, he said back to the voice. You'll always owe me for that. I wasn't even sixteen years old. Got an early start for you, Mother.

He turned the bottle up and took another swig. He wasn't a morning drinker by habit. Once it hit noon, sure, on occasion. It might be why his machine shop wasn't doing so well, but he would not admit it to himself. It was the economy, everything was now. America was shit and Sonny was just another sap caught in the stream of it. He pulled the cell phone from his belt and sent Charlotte a text message. It was early but he knew she would be up. They had decisions to make. It would all be over soon and Sonny Gaines would be on his way west somewhere. California looked good to him once, but not anymore. It was a fuck-liberal state again, not a place for real men like Sonny. Arizona maybe. They had deserts in Arizona, and Sonny planned to settle down away from everyone, just him and Shirls out there in no man's land where he could become someone else, the someone else he had wanted to be from the time his mother looked at him like he was the worst thing that ever happened to her. He could say the same, he thought, as he took a final swallow and screwed the lid back on. It washed away the bitter taste in his mouth that never went away. He would soon be settling up with his mother, closing the account out and leaving her to a fate he was certain held an unpleasant surprise. Everybody pays up, he knew. Everybody gets the knock at the door. He would not be in her life when it came.

# CHAPTER SEVENTEEN

Linda said nothing to them about the intruder when they gathered for breakfast just past eight o'clock. She had not been back to sleep, though she had returned to bed before the sun made its first appearance, sliding silently next to Kirsten. She knew from their time together that Kirsten slept soundly—too soundly for her own good, Linda thought. But that was just her; years of being on call at all hours of the day and night had made her someone who slept on the precipice, there where consciousness hovered. She also believed from her years in law enforcement that life can be unpredictable. Being fast asleep when someone was crawling through your window or picking the lock on your back door could prove fatal. She was prepared at all times, and this morning she was grateful for it.

Kyle said it had been one of the most restful nights in months, and Danny agreed.

"It's hard to get a good night's sleep with two cats in the bed who get all the sleep they need during the day," Kyle said, eating only half the French toast Linda made. It was delicious and he had not spared the maple syrup, but he didn't want to end their visit any heavier than he'd arrived.

"Smelly's the worst," Danny said. "You have to stop feeding her at three in the morning."

"It gets them to leave me alone when I'm at my computer at six."

"You get up at six?" Kirsten said, surprised.

"It's when I work on my photography. I'm a morning person. I have to head to work at eight-thirty and it's the only way I get things done."

"Speaking of your photography—"

"Let's not."

It was a touchy subject for Kyle. After the exhibit at the Katherine Pride Gallery last spring he found himself losing interest. It wasn't something he wanted to admit to himself; he'd been an avid shutterbug, as he called himself, for a decade, and realizing he no longer had the passion for it was upsetting to him. He knew the time was coming to either reinvigorate his love of photography, or start dating again, looking for a new passion. He liked to write, but would never call himself a writer. He had always been fascinated at other people's ability to paint, including his mother's since she had been widowed and started exploring her creative side. But he was no painter. What, then? He didn't know, and he didn't want to talk about it.

"Any homes to show today?" Kyle asked Kirsten, changing the subject.

Kirsten had taken her shower and dressed already. "No," she said. "We're closed to the public on Mondays."

"So you can spend the day with us!" said Danny.

Linda knew they would not be spending the day together, and for once she was glad of it. She had already made plans while she drank two cups of dark roast before sunup.

"Paperwork," Kirsten said. "Mondays is when everyone comes into the office to get things done. We have an admin, Stephanie, but she can only do so much. So we all go in and catch up before the grind starts again on Tuesday."

*The grind.* Linda had never heard Kirsten refer to her job as a grind before. "But you love your job," she said.

"Madeline has offered to buy me out. I'm considering it."

"Really?" Linda wondered if this had something to do with Kirsten's sudden willingness to consider life in the country.

"She likes the sound of McClellan and Powers without the McClellan."

"But do you like it?" asked Danny.

"I don't know yet, I just don't know. I've been in real estate for twenty years, I'm not sure what else I would do."

Kyle knew exactly how she felt. Not only had he lost the kind of interest in photography that kept him getting up at dawn, but he knew

Imogene would surely move on to something better soon. And while it had never officially been Landis and Callahan, the two had worked together for six years and he didn't know if he had the heart to be anyone else's assistant.

"I'm considering my options," Kirsten continued. "Maybe I do this on my own, or maybe I never sell homes again. Homes, townhouses, condos. Rentals. Madeline insisted we add rentals when the economy tanked. I'm tired of it all." She reached across the table and took Linda's hand. "So what were you doing up in the middle of the night?"

Linda hoped her blush didn't give her away. "I couldn't sleep, that's all. You know me."

"Up at the slightest sound, yes, I do. Was there a sound?"

Now Linda thought Kirsten might be playing with her. Had she woken up, too? Had she seen Linda take the gun from the nightstand and pad out quickly into the hallway? She didn't think so. Kirsten said what she thought, and if she knew what happened she would not be treating it so lightly.

"Only my aunt's ghost," Linda said. "She walks the house room to room at night ..."

"Stop!" Kyle said. He didn't care for talk of ghosts, especially not when he was sleeping in an attic. He had imagined many monsters in his grandmother's attic, many foes he had barely vanquished in their fights to the death.

"Well," said Kirsten, pushing away from the table. "I hope she likes me. A lot."

She smiled at Linda and rose from her chair. "Time to do some paperwork."

Ten minutes later they had all finished. Kirsten had brushed her teeth and put on a light fall jacket, ready for her day. She said goodbye with a lingering kiss and hugged Linda longer than she had since they'd first met. "Everything's going to be fine, my love."

*My love.* There it was again. Linda thought it might be just one term of endearment as they tried them out with each other. *My love. Sweetie. Pumpkin.* No, not pumpkin, that was out. She was happy to let Kirsten try it on for size and if it fit, Linda would proudly wear it. She watched at the kitchen door as Kirsten drove off down Lockatong Road. Then fear struck her as she wondered if the car from last night had headed off down the highway or was waiting out of sight. She had the impulse to go running down the drive, waving in warning behind Kirsten's car. But she let it go. It was her imagination—to a point. The intruder had been real, the taillights had been real.

"Listen," Linda said, turning back into the kitchen. "I've got a couple stops in mind today, if you're up for it."

"It's a rhetorical question," Danny said. "Of course he's up for it. But I'll stay here. I want to get to know your aunt better."

"Stop with the ghosts!" Kyle said. He put the last of the dishes into the dishwasher, filled it with soap and turned it on. "Danny leaves the crime solving to me."

"We don't just have to solve this one," Linda said. "We have to stop it from spreading, soon. I'll tell you about it in the car. Unless …"

"No," said Danny, "I don't want to hear about it. The less I know, the less I worry."

"So where are we going first?" Kyle asked, washing his hands in the sink.

"I need a good lawn man," she said. "I think a stop at Sly Mullen's house is in order."

"Does he know you're coming?"

She thought of last night and how close they'd come to disaster. Had the intruder made it any further into the house one of them would be dead this morning, and Linda knew it would not be her. "Let's hope not," she said. "They usually don't know I'm coming."

Kyle felt a chill course through him. He knew Detective Linda Sikorsky was tough, but he had never heard her speak with such cool determination. Something had happened, and the sooner they were in the car, the sooner she would tell him.

"Let's hit the road, then," he said, wiping his hands on a dishtowel and heading to the closet for a sweater. He didn't know if the cold he felt was from the open kitchen door or the tone in Linda's voice.

Linda got a jacket from the coat closet and slipped the .45 into a pocket. "I'll start the car," she said, heading outside and closing the door behind her.

Kyle and Danny were left in the kitchen. Kyle could tell by Danny's expression he was unhappy with this turn of events. "We'll be fine," he said.

"You almost died on a rooftop in SoHo the last time the two of you got together. I'm sure you'll be fine."

"We're not after a crazed serial killer, it's different this time."

"Is it?

Kyle went to Danny and held him. In that moment he thought of time passing. Seven years and then some. A year from now they would be married. And then? Then it was a matter of walking the road together until one of them reached the end. You're so damn maudlin, Kyle thought. Please stop.

He kissed Danny goodbye and headed to the car. Danny went to the window and watched them. They sat talking in the car for several minutes and Danny wondered what Linda was telling Kyle.

He felt something brush at his ankles and for an instant thought the cats were there, doing their best to trip him. No, no cats. No ghosts but memories. No reason to worry too much. He locked the kitchen door and headed upstairs, deciding to rest a bit more before calling his mother-in-law. It was a call he dreaded but had to make. There would be only one boss at Margaret's Passion, and his name was Danny.

# CHAPTER EIGHTEEN

Linda drove Kyle the scenic route down Lockatong Road, away from Route 651. He'd never gone this way, though it was simply a matter of turning right out of the driveway instead of left.

"I thought you'd like to see the back roads," she said, steering the car slowly along. The trees seemed to darken in their colors by the day. "There's a shooting range just up the road."

"Like, handguns?"

"No, like hunters. Rifles and shotguns mostly. Maybe skeet, I've never been there. You don't have to go there to hear the place."

That explained the booms Kyle heard throughout the day. He hadn't asked what they were.

As she headed along past the well-spaced neighboring homes she told him about the intruder.

"I don't know what spooked him," she said. "He must have heard me getting up."

"I thought nobody heard you." Kyle knew Detective Linda prided herself on being ready at a moment's notice and always maintaining the upper hand.

"Well, he heard something, and out he went like a scared rabbit."

She told him she had stayed up after that, at least for another hour before creeping quietly back to bed. During that time she had used her laptop in the living room, using a small desk lamp to see by, and looked up Quinidine online.

"It's for heart arrhythmia," she said. "Clarence …"

"I know about that. I was meaning to tell you, but I have no idea what it means. The tea man from the market told me Clarence was looking for a natural remedy. There is none, at least not that you can steep in a cup of hot water."

"It causes stomach cramps."

"Tea?"

"No," said Linda. "Quinidine. Stomach cramps are one of the side effects, at least at the beginning. Someone very likely treated Abigail Creek to a few pills to make her sick for a night. It was all the time they needed."

"We know it wasn't Justine," Kyle said.

"Do we?"

Kyle couldn't imagine Justine being involved in her mother's murder, but he heard Linda out.

"Maybe Abigail went to the Famers Market to confront Justine about her secret relationship with Clarence and Justine invited her for a spiked cappuccino on the front patio."

"And she just happened to have a few of her father's heart pills on hand."

Linda thought about it a moment. Kyle was right, it didn't work. But it didn't rule out the pills as the cause of Abigail's illness, either. It just meant someone else in the family had pilfered them and given them to Abi without her knowing it.

"I'm curious to know what the man who goes unnoticed, noticed," Linda said, turning left at the end of the road. "If anything. We'll know soon enough, he's only a mile up the road."

They settled in for the rest of the short drive in silence, each thinking on the intruder, the Quinidine, how they were connected, and who had connected them.

"What if it's not one person?" Kyle said suddenly.

"I've thought about that. It must be more than one, since the family was at dinner when Abigail was killed."

Linda saw the house she was looking for just around a corner, tucked quietly behind a row of trees. She had not called ahead and was thankful when she saw Sly Mullen's truck in the driveway, a battered Dodge pickup with a large riding lawnmower in the back. This must be the place.

Sly Mullen knew someone was there when he felt the house vibrate slightly. He'd been in the small room he used as an office, working on that month's invoicing. He had sixteen accounts in the surrounding county and, as usual, a half dozen of them had not paid for September. He sent out reminder notices every month, wording them carefully to be as nice as he could. He'd lost a few steady customers that year and couldn't afford to lose more. Finding new ones was a challenge, especially in an economy that had been stuck in neutral for several years now. Some of the families now had teenage sons they put into service on their lawns. And then there were the Mexicans, Dominicans, Salvadorans, wherever they came from. He didn't fault them—a man has to feed his family. He faulted his main competitor, Oscar Savidge, who'd managed to expand the last decade with an army of hedgers and leaf blowers all speaking Spanish as he put them to work for $4 an hour. Meanwhile Oscar charged by the job and pocketed the significant difference between what the landowners paid him and what he gave his men. *Landowners.* The word stuck in Sly's throat. He should have been one of them by now. He should be paying the next Sly Mullen to cut his grass, trim his hedges and pull his weeds. But the world was unfair. Most people just wanted to imagine otherwise.

Sly's wife Becky looked out the living room window and watched as a tall woman and a man got of the their car and walked to the door. "Sly!" she called. "Somebody's here!"

He knew that. He'd felt them arrive. He set aside an invoice to the Murphys on Slow Hill Road and headed for the front door. He didn't care much for John Murphy, an insufferable prick who called every week with a complaint. If Murphy dropped him, Sly could live with that. He was getting tired of the yard business. It didn't seem like the kind of tradition you handed down from father to son, but that's what had happened. Until now. Sly Mullen was determined his son Jeremy would not mow anyone's lawn, not for a living anyway.

"Can I help you?" Sly said as he opened the door and looked out at Linda and Kyle.

Linda quickly took stock of the man. He was shorter than she'd imagined, having only seen him from a distance. He stood just over five feet, with light brown hair and a sloped nose that reminded her of Bob Hope, or the Tin Man from the Wizard of Oz. He was wearing a loose red t-shirt and very worn jeans, and the ruddy complexion Linda had noticed from the back porch on CrossCreek Farm seemed permanent, the kind of burnt red that comes from working in the sun all your life.

"Hello," Linda said. "I'm Linda Sikorsky ..."

"I know who you are."

Linda was taken aback. It appeared she wasn't the only one who did a little research on her neighbors.

Seeing her surprise, Sly said, "You're Celeste Dickerson's niece. I seen you at her house a time or two, from the road. I drive around these roads all the time, and people talk, it's just their nature. Sorry she passed."

"Thank you," Linda said. "She spoke highly of you."

"Come in." Sly opened the door wide, motioning Linda and Kyle into the entryway. "And there's no need to lie. I doubt old Celeste ever said a word about me."

It was true, of course. Celeste had mowed her own lawn until she felt too old to do it, then she'd had a volunteer from her church, a good boy named Davie. There was no reason to hire a yard man. Linda knew her aunt must have known about Sly, everyone did in a small community like this, but she'd had no reason to speak about him and she didn't.

Becky Mullen came in from the living room, which required little more than a half dozen steps. She was a pretty woman, noticeably taller than her husband, with straw blonde hair she wore tied back and chocolate brown eyes. Coming up behind her, shy but curious, was a little boy Linda judged to be about eight years old.

"I'm Becky, Sly's wife. And this is Jeremy, but don't expect him to say anything. He's been taught not to speak to strangers."

She said it with no ill intent and Linda took none. It was good the boy had been taught well. Linda knew that strangers, especially ones with smiles on their faces, could be very dangerous.

"We'd offer you coffee," Sly said as he closed the door behind them, "but it depends on how long you're gonna stay. You need a lawn man? Or you on some other kind of mission? And who's the guy with you, quiet as Jeremy?"

Kyle blushed. He'd been silent, letting Linda take the lead and not wanting to say anything that would make Mullen suspicious. "I'm Kyle," he said, putting out his hand and shaking. "Kyle Callahan, I'm visiting from New York City."

"I see," Sly said. "Becky, would you mind making us a cup of coffee? I got a feeling they're not here to talk about weeds ... unless it's the people kind. Got plenty of those in Kingwood Township and nobody ever seems to pull 'em up. So come on in, Linda and Kyle. We can sit in the living room and see what it is you're really here for."

Linda liked this man. He said what he thought. He led Kyle and Linda into the living room while Becky set about making a pot of coffee, with little Jeremy close on her heels.

Linda and Kyle settled into a well-worn couch while Sly eased onto a large matching chair. The living room was small, in keeping with the rest of the house. The furniture had the look of a family living within its means; it was old, but clean and comfortable. Linda saw not a speck of dust anywhere, and guessed that Becky Mullen was a stay-at-home-mom.

"So," said Sly, as Becky brought them three cups of coffee on a tray, with milk and sugar on the side. "I know what brings you here—the death of Abigail Creek. What I don't know is why you think I have anything to tell you."

Linda waited a moment while Becky went to each of them and offered the tray. She began to wonder if the Mullens were religious; Becky Mullen had a cheerful subservience to her, acting not so much as a hostess as the help. But there was no indication it was forced or unwanted, no signal that Becky would have it any other way. Once Linda and Kyle had their coffee set on wooden TV trays Becky smiled, said, "Enjoy," and left the room. Little Jeremy had remained in the doorway, waiting on his mother. He followed her back into the kitchen, giving them as much privacy as could be had in a house this size.

Linda leaned forward. "Justine Creek referred to you—and I'm paraphrasing here—as someone who goes unnoticed but notices everything."

"Did she," Sly said, no reaction in his voice to the comment.

"I'm hoping she's right. Not about going unnoticed, but about what you might have observed lately at CrossCreek Farm."

Sly sipped his coffee, then set it on the arm of his chair. "Oh, I seen plenty over the years there." He hesitated, and Linda thought it might be from a sense of breaking some confidence.

"I don't much care what they think of me, if they notice me or not," he said. "I take care of their lawn, they pay me, that's as far as the loyalty goes."

"So did you?" Kyle asked. "Notice anything?"

"Well," Sly said, and this time he smiled. "The son's got a gambling habit. He's been spotted with the local loan shark enough times to confirm it, you don't need me for that. The daughter Justine hasn't been around the farm for some years, but meets with old man Clarence on the side. You can confirm that too."

"Is that something Abigail wasn't happy about?" Linda asked, already knowing the answer.

"That's putting it mildly. Abi Creek was more than unhappy. Now, I didn't get close enough to hear anything, you know. I'm just the unnoticed guy." He smiled again. "But I'd say Abi was close to killin' somebody over it. Looks like they got to her first."

"Why weren't you at the wake?" Kyle asked.

The smile quickly vanished from Sly's face. "I'm not a family member. I don't associate with these people. I cut their grass. Not one of them is a friend, they ain't never been to my house. Hell, I don't think most of 'em know I got a son—who won't be cutting their grass when he gets older. That's a family tradition that stops with me."

Linda detected bitterness in the words. After a moment she said, "What about Charlotte Gaines?"

"What about her?"

"It's an odd arrangement. The other woman practically moves into the house while Abigail was still there. All of them acting like it was some kind of non-traditional family."

"Oh, it was non-traditional, all right."

"Did you ever notice anything?" Kyle asked.

"I noticed the two of them on the back patio, about a week ago," Sly said. "Abigail and Charlotte, arguing. Looked like it might even get physical, but it didn't."

"You weren't able to hear anything?"

"From twenty yards away? Not hardly. All I heard was my mower. It gets pretty loud with me on top of it. Doctor said I've probably lost some hearing from the years of it. No, I didn't hear nothing."

Linda thought about it all. It didn't seem Sly Mullen would be able to tell them much more, given that he never heard anything, or did and was refusing to say what. She suddenly felt awkward in this man's home, as if she had invaded it, and in a way she had. They had arrived unannounced, uninvited, and, she gathered, unwelcome.

"Well, Mr. Mullen," she said, finishing only half her coffee and putting it on the TV tray. "We thank you for your time."

"It's about all you got from me," he said. "Sorry I couldn't tell you more. If I was you, I'd have a another talk with Justine."

"I think we just might do that." Linda rose from the sofa. Kyle put his coffee down and stood as well, followed immediately by Sly. Their visit had come to an end.

Sly walked them to the door. Wherever Becky and Jeremy had gone, they were out of sight.

"Listen," Linda said as Sly opened the door for them.

"Let me guess, you need someone for your yard."

"Yes, yes I do."

"I knew your aunt. She was a good lady, and I never held it against her she got some kid from her church to do the lawn. I would too if somebody offered. You give it some thought, and if you really want me to take care of the place for you, you obviously know how to reach me."

Linda nodded, not sure what else to say. They had learned little, but the information about a heated argument between Abigail and Charlotte was a solid lead.

As she and Kyle were about to leave, she turned back to Sly. "The Mullens and the Creeks, you go way back from what Caroline said. Your father, your grandfather ..."

"We go back," he said from the doorway. "My great-grandfather Jacob worked for old man Davis. That was the owner of the place before Harlan Creek got hold of it."

It was an odd way to phrase it: *got hold of it.* "Harlan and my great-grandfather both worked for Davis. He left the place to Creek and we been working the land ever since. But like I said, that's gonna stop with me. Jeremy won't ever get grass stains on him if I have anything to say about it. My boy won't go unnoticed." He smiled, and Linda saw in it a weariness. This was a man who was tired of tending other people's lawns, as tired of doing it as he was of being the son of a man who had done it before him.

"Well, Mr. Mullen, thank you again. We really appreciate your taking time with us."

"My pleasure," Sly said, with the casual emptiness of the many times Linda had said, "I'm sorry for your loss." It was just something you told people under the circumstances.

She and Kyle walked to the car. Sly did not wait for them to reach it before closing the door behind them.

As they buckled in, Kyle asked, "Where to now, Detective?"

"I'd like to thank Justine Creek again for that lovely painting." Linda pushed the dashboard button that started her car. She was still getting used to a keyless world.

"You think she has more to tell us?"

"I don't doubt that. I think she may have quite a bit more to say."

Linda put the car in drive and pulled out onto the road. They would be making their second visit to the Famers Market since Kyle and Danny arrived. The way things were going, Kyle would be happy if it was the last time he ever saw the place.

# CHAPTER NINETEEN

Linda had forgotten the Stockton Farmers Market was only open Friday through Sunday, a lapse she regretted as she turned onto Bridge Street and realized her mistake. Parking was not a problem on Monday, since no one was there. She and Kyle had gone over their conversation with Sly Mullen several times on the short drive from his house, and she was hoping Justine Creek could shed more light on what little they'd learned. She was especially interested in the history of CrossCreek Farm after Sly referred to Harlan Creek as having "got hold of" the property. It wasn't how people usually referred to something freely given.

They needed to stop and think, so Linda pulled into a parking spot despite the Market being closed. "It doesn't look like we'll be talking to Justine," she said. "At least not here."

Kyle had noticed people sitting outside the Stockton Inn eating lunch. Another month and they wouldn't be able to do that, unless they enjoyed eating their meals in winter coats. He looked at his watch: it was just past noon, and he was feeling hungry. "Let's have lunch," he said. "We're already here, and I can take something back for Danny."

At first Linda thought it would take precious time away from their mission—though she had not yet defined it—but after a moment she agreed. This was as good a place as any to focus, look back over what they'd learned, and plan any next moves. "Sure," she said, and she put the car in park.

As they got out, Kyle glanced across the street at the gas station and stopped short. "Isn't that ..."

"It is," Linda said. There on the side of the station stood Charlotte Gaines, wearing a black leather coat and a baseball cap. Beside her was a young man on a motorcycle. He had on a denim jacket, and he was holding a helmet under his arm as he propped himself up on his left leg. The two appeared to be in a heated discussion.

"Who do you suppose she's talking to?" Kyle asked.

"No idea. We can't ask Justine."

"If she would even know." Then, "Don't look!"

Kyle quickly turned toward the Inn across the street. He started walking toward it, waving for Linda to follow. "I think they saw us," he said, smiling to mask his words. It was unlikely they could be heard this far away but he wasn't taking any chances.

Linda followed along, quickly memorizing the man they'd seen with Charlotte, what he was wearing, and the motorcycle. It wasn't like most they saw in this area, a popular riding route for big bikes. They were the bane of the neighborhood, roving in packs on weekends on and around the many country roads and highways. She knew it well from New Hope, where they gathered in a sort of hive and raised the decibel level to an ear-shattering roar. This motorcycle was a racer; whoever the young man was, he liked to travel fast. They reached the road and waited for oncoming traffic to stop.

It was too late; Charlotte had seen them. Sonny had seen them, too, but he didn't know who they were. He'd left his car back at his shop, telling his mother he'd already gotten rid of it. He'd never gotten a look at the woman who almost found him in her house, nor did he know how lucky that made him—had he seen Linda Sikorsky up close he might well be dead now.

They found a table on the front porch and ordered a light lunch, with another to take home. At first Kyle wanted to go inside where it was warmer, but Linda tugged him over to an outside table. She preferred being able to observe the comings and goings. The Farmers Market might be closed but Stockton was open for business. Already they had seen something very interesting. By the time they sat down Charlotte and the man were gone, somehow by a back route since neither passed them. Linda took it to be deliberate.

As Kyle was about to take a bite of his roasted beet salad, he looked up and saw Clara the muffin lady coming out of the Inn. She was alone and either knew people here or had come for lunch. "Look," he said, nodding toward the front door.

Linda turned and saw her. On instinct she called out, "Clara! Clara! How nice to see you!"

Clara Presley knew the pair only from sight. She remembered them going outside the market with Justine while she kept on eye on Justine's stall. She remembered them, too, from Abigail Creek's wake. She had no idea why they would be happy to see her, but Clara was more polite than suspicious and she walked over to the table. She was glad all the tables were for two and there was nowhere to sit; she did not want to be asked to join them.

Clara had turned sixty-two last July but knew she looked older. It was genetic. All the women in her family appeared at least ten years older than they were. It was why so many people thought of her as an old lady. She didn't feel like an old lady, but neither did she feel like telling them she wasn't. She was wearing jeans and a bright green sweater, red sneakers her granddaughter had given her. Did anyone still call them sneakers, she wondered, as she smiled at Linda and Kyle. "Nice to see you, too," she said, "though I can't say I know you. Do you like the painting?"

For a moment Linda didn't know what she was talking about, then realized it was the painting she'd bought from Justine, the one that depicted the road in front of her house.

"Yes," Linda said. "Yes I do, very much. In fact I was going to stop by and tell Justine how happy I am to have it in my aunt's house." There it was again: *my aunt's house.* She needed to stop doing that; it was her house now.

"We're closed Monday through Thursday, as you can see."

"As we can see," said Kyle.

"Well, folks, it was nice running into you. Justine will be back …"

"Actually," Linda said, "I was hoping to talk to you."

This was news to Kyle. He had no idea what they could learn from Clara the muffin lady, but he knew he was about to find out.

"Can you join us for some coffee?"

"I don't drink coffee, and there's nowhere to sit."

"Of course there is," Linda said. She quickly turned around to the table behind her where a man was having lunch by himself. "May I?" she said, and without waiting for his reply she took the empty chair across from him and dragged it around to their table.

Clara stared at the chair, trying to decide if this was a bad idea. They were in the open, with plenty of witnesses. It wasn't going to hurt her to sit a few minutes; she had nowhere to go, anyway, except back to her empty house. It had been too big for one person ever since her husband Henry died, but she had stayed there alone six years now. She might as well enjoy the company. She eased into the chair and set her purse on the porch beside her.

"It was so sad about Abigail," she said. The waitress came by but Clara waved her away. She had just eaten and wanted nothing to drink.

"Very sad," said Linda. She wondered if Clara knew they had found Abigail on the road. If she did she was not saying, and Linda was not going to tell her.

"I'd never been to CrossCreek Farm before," Linda continued. "Only to drive past it. It's quite a spread."

"Yes, well …" Clara's response was hesitant, as if she did not want to speak ill of the place. "I can't say I've ever been there, either. But Abi was always so nice to me, it was only right I say my goodbyes."

Linda wasn't sure how to proceed. She wanted to ask more, but had the sense she would need to be careful. "Is there something about the farm that makes you uncomfortable?"

Clara regretted sitting now. She didn't know these people and should have just waved and walked on. "No," she said finally, and Linda knew she was hiding something.

Acting as nonchalant as possible, Linda took a bite from her own salad and said, "The place is big for my tastes. I like my house—my aunt's house—did you know her?"

"Celeste? Oh my, yes. What a lovely woman. And she was very proud of you." Clara had just realized who she was talking to, but it didn't make Linda any less of a stranger. It was true she had never met the detective from New Hope, but she had heard Celeste brag on her many times.

"My aunt never said anything about CrossCreek Farm. I just knew she didn't much care for the place, either." Linda was off script now, if there had ever been one. Her aunt had never mentioned the farm in any context.

Clara thought a moment, then leaned in and lowered her voice. "I don't know what the opposite of hallowed ground is, but that place is it."

"Really?" Linda said, feigning surprise. A lot could be learned in conspiratorial tones. "That's what my aunt said, in so many words. She said the place was cursed."

Clara was more relaxed now. She remembered Celeste Dickerson fondly, and if Celeste had talked openly to her niece about the stories, she could, too. "My grandmother always told me to stay clear of CrossCreek Farm," she said.

"Your grandmother?" Kyle said.

"Oh yes. The farm's been around a long time, you know."

"I didn't know," Linda said. "I just know they make an excellent Pinot Grigio!"

"I couldn't say," said Clara. "I don't drink. But my grandmother warned us off that place when we were kids. That wasn't as long ago as you might think." She fussed with her gray hair, wondering if they, too, saw her as an old woman. "'Whatever grows there, grows in the shadows,' she always said."

"Do you know why she said that?" asked Linda.

Clara shrugged. It had been many years since her grandmother told them stories. All she knew then was that her grandmother was a goddess, and children do what goddesses tell them. She had never gone to CrossCreek Farm until the wake yesterday, and she would never be back.

"There's always been stories," she said.

"Stories?"

"About the land, how it came to be Harlan Creek's. I can't speak to the truth of it, so I won't. But you go back ninety years or so and something wasn't right. Not about the way old Randall Davis died, not about any of it."

"Who was Randall Davis?" Linda asked. The less she appeared to know, the more she might find out.

"Randall Davis was the original owner of the property."

"How did he die?" Linda took another bite of her salad as if they were having a casual conversation.

"Down a well," Clara said. "A well he knew was there. A well he'd been to many times—so my grandmother told me. Never made sense. He wasn't some kid playing where he wasn't supposed to be. He was an old man by then and there just wasn't any way he was going to fall down his own well. But he did, and that was that."

"So your grandmother told you," Kyle said.

Clara stared at him, not sure if he was being smart.

"Is that how Harlan Creek ended up with the land?" asked Linda.

"It is. And it's been CrossCreek Farm ever since." Clara was tired of the conversation and wanted to be gone. She had the uneasy feeling she had been invited to sit with them for this very reason, to tell them things they didn't know. It didn't spoil her opinion of Linda, such as it was; Celeste was a kind woman, but nobody's fool, and if she said her niece was A-one, then it had to be. But still, Clara had said more than she ever intended to, and she was finished.

"I need to get home now," she said, sliding her chair back and picking up her purse. "It's been nice visiting with you."

"You as well, Clara," Linda said. "I'm sure I'll be seeing much more of you at the market."

"I'm sure. Take care now." Clara walked off, leaving them to finish their lunch.

"We're getting closer," Linda said. She motioned to their waitress for a check.

"We are?" Kyle wasn't finished with his lunch but knew it would not be good to slow their momentum.

"Think about it. Randall Davis falls down a well on his own property. Harlan Creek 'gets hold of' the land."

"But what does any if it have to do with Abigail Creek?"

"I've thought from the beginning that Abigail wasn't killed for who she was, but for what she knew."

"It sounds like everyone else knew it, too."

"Ah," Linda said, taking the check from the waitress and waiting for her to leave. "Everyone *thought* it. But someone could prove it."

"Abigail."

Linda took a credit card from her wallet and set it on top of the check. Lunch was on her. It was the least she could do, especially given that Danny would have to wait awhile longer for his. They needed to make another stop.

"I take it we're not going back to the house," Kyle said.

"Flemington," Linda said. "The Hunterdon County Clerk's Office. They say where there's a will there's a way. I think it may be literal in this case."

"They don't have wills at a county clerk's office."

"No, but they have signatures."

Kyle thought about it, then guessed what Linda had in mind. "If it's a deed you're looking for, Randall Davis was dead when it changed hands. Dead men don't sign over their property."

"He was very much alive when he bought it," she said. "It's the living I'm looking for. At least before he fell down a well."

The waitress swooped in and took the check and credit card. Kyle did not protest or pull out his wallet in the universal gesture of pretending to pay. He and Danny had spent lavishly on dinner in New Hope and he was happy to let Linda get lunch. He picked up Danny's salad to go and hoped it wasn't wilted by the time they got back to the house.

Two minutes later they were walking back to the car, Linda looking around for a man on a motorcycle. Something told her he was not far away.

# CHAPTER TWENTY

onny made it back to his machine shop in record time. He'd been careless on the road, weaving in and out of cars well above the speed limit. He didn't care. Freedom was just beyond the horizon, and as he sped along the highway he could see it getting closer. Twenty-four hours from now he would be gone, behind the wheel of his beloved Mustang with Shirls in the passenger seat cackling at some stupid magazine. He was not about to get rid of his car, he loved it too much for that. Instead he was getting rid of Trenton and CrossCreek Farm and all of New Jersey. He'd take his car and his girlfriend and fuck everybody he ever knew here. All he needed was Shirls, as empty-headed as she was most of the time. She loved him, though, and she loved her magazines. She enjoyed reading about the sad, sordid lives of celebrities. She believed she had it better, that being nobody was preferable to the awful things stars did to themselves. She also believed nobodies had the last laugh. Sonny certainly planned on it; he would laugh all the way to the Mojave, smoking joints and sipping beer from a Coke can in case they passed a few cops on the road. He hadn't been caught yet and thought he never would be.

His mother had told him to get out now, toss Shirley on the back of his bike and hightail it out of Dodge. He was sure she hoped they wouldn't get far before spilling the bike and dying under the wheels of a big rig. That was just the sort of thing Charlotte wanted and Sonny knew it. He had been a liability to her all his life, except when she had a mess she needed cleaned up or he could provide her with some other service. He was like a prop to his mother, or a hammer she kept in a drawer in the basement and only took out when she had a nail to pound.

He never should have killed the old woman. Hell, he never should have gone to the house. Why did they call it a farm anyway? It wasn't a farm. It was a big-ass, ugly, flat house on too much land for any one family. The Creeks weren't nobodies, that was for certain, and they made sure everybody knew it. Maybe Shirls was right. Maybe misfortune takes special pleasure in the downfall of the rich, famous and powerful. The lady detective wasn't any of those things, but she was unfinished business. His mother told him who she was and that she was like a snake easing up slowly in the grass to wrap itself around them if they weren't careful. He'd been careful, too, getting into the house quiet as a ghost. The thought made him chuckle; what in the world had scared him like that? He wasn't one for a guilty conscience, but it's the only explanation he'd come up with since last night. Some part of him felt guilty for running Abigail Creek down like that. It was a coward's way to kill, and for it she'd come back for just a minute to stare him down. It hadn't looked like her, but who knew what spooks looked like until they saw one?

He rolled his bike into the shop and pulled the big sliding door down behind him. He'd tried to make a go of it, he really had. But times were hard, everybody knew that. He got behind on the rent, behind on his taxes, behind on everything until he was just about to find himself locked out with some notice from the Sheriff plastered to his door. Too fucking late, he thought, heading for the refrigerator he kept in the shop. It was mid-afternoon and well past time for a brew or three. He'd keep a lid on it, he had to. His unfinished business wouldn't stay that way much longer. He had one last mission, this one for himself, and he needed his wits about him. But not right now. He could have a six pack if he wanted to and still be fine by the time he had to head out.

Charlotte didn't know about this. Sonny smiled at the thought of her seeing it on the news tomorrow morning. It would make the news, too. The bitch was a retired cop for godsake. They'll talk about that one, they surely will.

He chugged his beer in a half dozen straight swallows and grabbed a can of peanuts from a tool shelf. He felt no sorrow whatsoever leaving his shop. It smelled like failure, something he was never willing to breathe too long. Sonny Gaines was a winner, it just took a few tries sometimes.

He'd set up a new shop when they got where they were going. Or maybe he'd do something else altogether. Maybe he'd become a cop! Wouldn't that beat all. Kill a cop and six months later be one. He liked that idea.

He felt his cell phone vibrate and yanked it off his belt. He always kept it on vibrate, hating the sound of telephones. Was that what they were even called anymore? He hadn't heard anyone say the word in a long time. He held the phone up and saw an incoming call from Shirley. He let it go to voicemail. He didn't feel like talking to her right now. By sunrise he'd be listening to her yammer all the way across the damn country.

He tossed his phone on a worktable, took the can of peanuts and headed to a small couch he kept in the shop for all those long nights he spent working, when he had work. It was a ratty thing, just barely long enough to accommodate him. He didn't care. He wanted a nap and this was as good a place as any to take it. One last nap on his last day in this shithole. Then it was freedom, clear and beautiful and as wide open to him as the sky. Sonny Gaines was going to fly away into it and never look back.

# CHAPTER TWENTY-ONE

nown as "The Keeper of the Records," the Hunterdon County Clerk's Office is one of the oldest offices in the state of New Jersey. The county itself is the 14th most-populace in the state. It's also among the wealthiest counties in the country and retains a distinctly conservative political identity. Every election cycle the properties are dotted with lawn signs and bumper stickers for whatever Republican is running for office.

The Clerk's Office is located on Main Street in Flemington, which is where Linda drove them after leaving the Stockton Inn. Kyle only knew Flemington from driving through it. He knew where the shopping outlet was, and the McDonald's where he and Danny would stop as a halfway point on their trips to New Hope. He knew the dreaded circles, too, where cars wound quickly around, the drivers often hesitant as they tried to figure out who had the right of way at each yield sign. Once in awhile there would be an accident as a driver guessed wrongly and ended up circling into the side of another car.

Linda parked on a side street and hunted in her glove box for the roll of quarters she always kept there.

"Do you think they'll even have a deed that old?" Kyle said, unbuckling his seatbelt.

"I'm betting they do. That's why we're going to the Hall of Records. It's a good thing they used paper back then and not flash drives."

Paper was still in wide use, of course. Notaries were everywhere, and anything legal was still signed with a pen, but Linda assumed the day would come when everything was digital. You could sign a credit card transaction on an iPhone now; it was only a matter of time.

They got out of the car and Linda dropped in five quarters, giving them just over an hour. She locked the car and they headed into the Clerk's Office. It wasn't much of a building, given its importance and stature. It stands only two stories tall and looked to Linda more like an old schoolhouse than a repository of records. She had imagined it more like the Smithsonian, where her mother had taken her several years after her father was killed. But those were the daydreams of a child, and as they entered the building she realized most clerk's offices were probably like this, faded brown brick and bureaucratic.

Upon entering, Linda asked the security officer guarding the front door where the deeds office was. "Second floor, three doors to the right," he said, with as little emotion as one would expect from a man answering the same questions all day long.

They took the stairs, turned right and found themselves in a small room with a front desk. Behind the desk was another man, busying himself with paper. He was young, maybe twenty-five, which surprised Linda for some reason. She thought everyone who worked here would be like the building: squat, older and disinterested.

"Can I help you?" the young man said, looking up over his glasses without raising his head. At least the glasses fit her stereotype.

"I'm looking for a record," she replied.

He raised his head then, too high, and peered at them down his nose. "I assumed that," he said. "This is the Hall of Records. What sort of record are you looking for?"

"A deed."

"A deed."

Linda wondered if he was going to repeat everything she said. "A property deed from about, oh, 1900, in there somewhere."

On the way from Stockton they had talked about what Clara told them. Linda calculated that Harlan Creek was probably born some time around 1900, maybe a bit earlier, just about when Randall Davis was taking ownership of what would become his dairy farm. Clara said he was an older man when he fell down his own well, so a quick calculation on the drive over led Linda to believe Davis probably got the property somewhere close to the turn of the century.

"What property is in question?" the man asked.

"Well," said Linda, "it's now called CrossCreek Farm. Before that it was a dairy farm owned by a man named Randall Davis. I'm looking for the deed that gave him the land."

"Let me see ..." The man turned to a laptop on the desk and began a search. At least that part of it was in the modern era—everything was on computer now, and Linda knew that if they didn't have all their records digitized yet, they would before too long.

After a moment the man looked at them and said, "Ah, yes, here it is. 1902, the property was purchased from the county at auction by one Randall Elijah Davis."

"May I see the deed?"

He looked at her as if she were not the brightest child in the schoolhouse. "I don't have the deed," he said. "I have the record, and I can't very well snatch it off the computer screen and give it to you, now can I?"

Linda decided he may be young, but he had the soul of an old, squat, disinterested clerk's office.

"I'd like a copy of the deed itself," she said.

He turned away from the computer and faced them. "You can fill out a record request form. You'll have a copy in two weeks."

"I can't wait two weeks."

"I'm sorry, Miss ..."

She hadn't been called 'Miss' in a very long time, but it gave her an opportunity. "Detective," she said. "Detective Linda Sikorsky, from the New Hope Police Department. We're investigating a murder."

Now the man was interested. He didn't get many murder investigations; in fact, this was his first. He was too young and inexperienced to ask for identification, something Linda was grateful for. All she had to show him was the gun in her jacket pocket, and she preferred not to let Kyle know she had it.

"Let me see what I can do," the man said. "Sissy?" he called out. For a moment Kyle was startled, wondering if the man had just uttered a slur, then he saw an elderly woman who looked more appropriate to the front desk of the Hall of Records scurry out from behind a row of file cabinets.

"Yes, Thomas," she said, sliding up to the desk.

*Thomas*, Linda thought. Of course he would insist on being called Thomas. Not Tom, certainly not Tommy. He was perfectly suited to the job, even if he was young enough to be her son.

"I'm going to the archives," he said.

Sissy's eyes widened. This was unusual! She looked at Linda and Kyle as if they must be terribly important people.

"I'll be back in fifteen minutes or so, please take over."

"Yes, Thomas." She planted herself firmly at the desk as if she were an armed guard instead of a short, frail old woman wishing she'd put enough money away not to spend her days here. Or maybe she's a volunteer, Linda thought. Maybe this gives her life purpose.

"Excuse me," Thomas said and disappeared through the back. Linda guessed the archives were in the basement, probably in a temperature-controlled environment. She hoped so, anyway, wanting the deed to still be legible.

"I hear you're a police detective," Sissy said to Linda after Thomas had gone.

"You did?"

Sissy blushed. "Well, I overheard it, not that I listen to other people's conversations, it's not my nature."

"I wouldn't think it was."

"So what's it like?" Sissy asked. She leaned in closer, anticipating stories of life on the streets as a beat cop. "Have you ever shot anyone?"

*Yes, and I might shoot you,* Linda thought, smiling at the woman. It was going to be a long fifteen minutes.

Thomas made good time and returned in exactly twelve and a half minutes. He was holding a photocopy.

"Here's your deed copy, Officer," he said as he came up behind Sissy. She looked disappointed; Linda had not shared any stories with her of corpses on the sidewalk or gun battles.

"Detective," Linda corrected him. "Homicide." It was purely for effect and she kept a straight face as Thomas and Sissy's eyes widened. A real life homicide detective was standing in front of them. "May I see the deed?"

All the while Kyle had been standing quietly to the side, enjoying himself.

Thomas handed her the copy, and there it was: the signature of Randall E. Davis, taking ownership of Land Parcel 27D. That was the only identification the property had then. The year was 1903. Randall Davis must have been about thirty when he bought the land that would become CrossCreek Farm on his death.

"What do I owe you?" Linda said, taking her wallet out. Records usually ran in the ten-dollar range, but maybe they'd gone up to twenty with inflation.

"This one's on me," Thomas said. "We support our heroes."

Linda winced. She was not a hero. Losing her life on the job had been a possibility early on when she rode a patrol car, and even now, as a trained police officer who might find herself in the wrong place at the wrong time, as her father had tragically discovered. But a hero? She regretted that everyone in uniform was now called that. The possibility of death came with the job, just like dying on the road was a possibility for every truck driver in the country. Heroes, to her mind, did heroic things. The one exception was her father. He had been a hero to her from the day she was born.

"Thank you, Thomas, thank you very much." Linda took the photocopy and carefully rolled it into a tube. "Now, if you'll excuse us…"

She and Kyle turned to leave.

"May I ask you something?" Thomas said as they were about to walk out.

Linda stopped at the door. "Sure, why not."

"Who was killed?"

Linda thought a moment. It couldn't hurt to tell him something, he had been so easily manipulated and so helpful. "An old woman on a country road," she said.

"Why was she killed?" Sissy asked.

Linda held up the photocopy. "For this."

The answer left the two office clerks perplexed but satisfied. They would both spend the rest of the day knowing they had helped bring justice to a world with too little of it.

Back at the car, as they were about to get in, Kyle asked, "Where to now, Detective?"

"Are you ever going to stop calling me that?"

Kyle pretended to think about it, then said, "Probably not."

Linda sighed, resigned to being Detective Linda forever, or at least as long as she knew Kyle Callahan.

"Home," she said. It was now mid-afternoon and she knew Kirsten was coming back soon. It was the second night in a row she would be staying at the house, and Linda knew it was Kirsten's way of getting used to it. Their next visit to CrossCreek Farm, where she believed she would find the crucial piece to the puzzle of Abigail Creek's murder, could wait till morning. Abigail had the patience of the dead now, and things were coming to a head. Linda would prefer to get there rested, ready and unexpected.

# CHAPTER TWENTY-TWO

Charlotte sat on the back patio with a glass of Scotch and water. It was a rare indulgence for her; alcohol had been ever-present in her childhood, brief as it was. A girl forced into pregnancy at fourteen cannot be said to have much of a childhood. The time between playing with dolls and giving birth had been short for her, and it had left her with a lifelong feeling of being robbed. Not just violated—that came in many forms for a woman—but deprived of something that had been hers for a moment. She could never get it back.

She wondered why this time of day was called the gloaming. She had no idea where the word came from, only that it meant the end of the day when the sky slowly darkened. It was a lovely word, and appropriately sad. It matched her mood as she stared out at the property that would soon be hers, assuming Sonny did as she told him and was long gone by morning. Him and his halfwit girlfriend Shirley. He'd never made a go of it with the machine shop. He would lose nothing if he left it all behind, but he stood to lose everything if he stayed.

Abigail was not supposed to die on the road, run down like an animal. She was supposed to die in the house, the victim of a burglary gone wrong. That was his first mistake and it had been a huge one. Then he got spooked at the house on Lockatong Road and failed to frighten off the detective. He wasn't supposed to kill anyone there, not unless it had been necessary, just … distract Linda Sikorsky with a break-in, send her off on another trail instead of the one Charlotte worried was quickly leading to her. She looked at her cell phone and considered calling Sonny to make sure they were well on their way. No, she thought, let them drive.

Let them drive without stopping until they reach a place no one will ever find them, and let them never come back.

She sipped her drink. Clarence had introduced her to Scotch, a taste she had acquired since their first clandestine meeting in a hotel in New York City. That's how far Clarence had insisted on going to make sure they would not be seen. It was early in his betrayal of Abigail, and Charlotte knew he had hoped it would just be a quick affair. Or longstanding; men had always wanted what they could get from Charlotte for as long as they could get it. But an affair, nothing more. Then he had fallen in love with her—she had seen to that— and now it had all come to this. Had Abigail simply taken Clarence's generous offer they would be going their separate ways soon, Abigail with enough money from the divorce to never worry about support- ing herself again, and Charlotte with Clarence and CrossCreek Farm. She'd made sure Caroline knew she and Rusty would be staying. This was not a war to fight on two fronts, and she was glad she'd made that play early on. Caroline was in her corner, however unwittingly. Rusty was another matter. While he couldn't prove anything, he valued his suspicions and had let Charlotte know he had them. He would have to be paid off when everything was settled. Charlotte would pay it, too. No price was as high as spending her life in prison for a murder she had ordered. Clarence, meanwhile, had no idea what was going on. Or at least the 'who' of it. Believing someone in your family killed your wife, no matter how much he wanted her gone, was not an easy thought to harbor. He preferred to think it had been random, that Abigail rode off in the night for reasons no one would ever under- stand and had been hit by a drunk driver. That was what he'd been telling himself the last three days. Charlotte reinforced his thinking, telling him repeatedly that they had all been at dinner, this was clearly a freak event. She knew he preferred believing her to thinking his son or his daughter-in-law (never Justine, of course, no never Justine) had done something unspeakable.

Charlotte picked up her glass and swirled the last of the melting ice. The funeral was Wednesday. Abigail would be laid to rest soon, and not long after that the death of Abigail Creek would fade into mystery. An accident of some kind. A convergence of events no one would ever understand but would accept in time. A tragedy. Life was full of them, as Charlotte well knew. She glanced at her phone again. She had told Sonny not to call her; she would call him. Now it was a matter of when. Charlotte finished her Scotch and set her glass down, thinking she may never speak to her son again. It would suit her just fine.

# CHAPTER TWENTY-THREE

Kyle and Danny were getting used to nights in the country. Kyle hadn't noticed the difference at first, but now it was evident. Gone were the sirens blaring down Lexington Avenue, five flights down from their apartment windows. No students from Baruch College clustering and chattering, moving about in a hive. No shouts or screams. Here on Lockatong Road they heard only night sounds, the kind you hear where there are no buildings or cars or frantic city movement.

The four of them were sitting in the kitchen with the window open. A moth circled the overhead lamp hanging down above the table. Kirsten had called ahead and told them not to cook, she was bringing dinner from Patsy's, an upscale diner in New Hope that had managed to survive nearly twenty years. Everybody loved Patsy's. There was a Patsy, just like there was a Margaret at Margaret's Passion, and she made comfort food deserving of the name: meatloaf drenched in pan gravy, sweet potato mash, sautéed green beans with garlic and bacon, and pecan pie. Kirsten had even stopped on the way back and bought vanilla ice cream to put on the pie, once it had been warmed in the microwave. It was the sort of meal you might eat at your grandmother's house, if your grandmother served the best home cooking in town.

The last three days had been full of surprises for Linda, some bad, some exceptionally good. One thing she was trying to figure out was Kirsten's sudden change of heart. Just two days ago Linda had been sure things were faltering. Kirsten had seemed averse to staying at the house, and Linda worried she had decided it had all been a mistake. And now ... now things were very different. Now Linda wondered if something happened to precipitate this change. Was Kirsten tired of her profession?

Did she really want McClellan and Powers to just be Powers Real Estate? And what would she do if she moved out here, honestly? She was not a country girl, of that Linda was certain.

"Amazing dinner," Danny said. "If it was the kind of food we served at Margaret's Passion I'd ask for the recipes."

"Patsy wouldn't give them to you anyway," Kirsten said. "Few trade secrets are as guarded as the ingredients of great meatloaf."

Kirsten made no objection when Linda and Kyle offered to clean up. She and Danny headed into the living room where Kirsten set about making the first fire of the season. Linda's aunt Celeste had made good use of her fireplace, relying on it to heat the house in winter and save on oil.

Taking plates to the sink to be rinsed and stacked in the dishwasher, Kyle said, "What's our next move? I know there is one."

"I want to see the will," Linda said, picking up silverware and glasses.

"You think it's a forgery."

"Somebody left that land to Harlan Creek, and it wasn't old Randall Davis."

"But you don't know that."

"I can't be certain, no. But you didn't ask that. You asked what the next move was."

Kyle rinsed the dishes and handed them off to Linda. "What if it's not a forgery? What if there is no will?"

"There's a will, there always is. And someone like Clarence Creek is going to have at least a copy of the document that makes him the owner of his own property. Whoever the executor of the estate was—if there was one—is long dead."

"What if there's only the deed?"

Linda sighed. "You're making this more difficult than it needs to be. If there's no will, then we keep digging. But let's just assume there is, for the sake of conjecture. If the signature's don't match we know the will is a fake. If they do match, or there's no will ..."

"Or Clarence simply tells you there isn't one. He's not under any obligation to show us anything."

"If he has it he'll produce it. That is a truly grieving man. I've met many in my time investigating the deaths of their loved ones. He didn't kill his wife."

"Does he know who did?"

"I have no idea. But I'm going to wager he knows why she was killed, and as terrible as grief is, we can use it to our advantage. I have a feeling guilt isn't very far from grief for Clarence Creek. The sooner we offer him a way to be free of it, the sooner we'll be at the end of this road."

"A road Abigail died on."

They finished up in the kitchen and joined Danny and Kirsten in the living room. The fire was going strong now, and they could smell it seeping into the room while smoke floated up into the chimney. Linda sat next to Kirsten on the couch and watched the flames for several minutes. She had never spent time with her aunt on a cold night. This was the first time she had seen logs burning in this fireplace. It warmed her and made her sad at the same time. She hoped wherever her aunt was she could see them all now, enjoying a fire where a year ago Celeste had been, watching the flames with a shawl around her shoulders. Thank you, Aunt, Linda thought as she slid close to Kirsten. She took Kirsten's hand and held it, wanting the moment to last forever.

Music was playing again in the bedroom. Kyle and Danny had gone up to bed an hour before. Linda and Kirsten had each read for awhile in bed, Linda scanning a magazine while Kirsten made it to the half-way mark in a biography of Ronald Reagan. Her political leanings were conservative in many respects and it gave the women something else in common. Linda had quickly discovered that being Republican in a gay crowd was often like being gay in a Republican one. It gave her another closet to come out of.

Linda knew something was on Kirsten's mind, so she set the magazine down on the floor beside her and waited. It didn't take long.

Kirsten slipped a bookmark between the pages and laid the book on the headboard shelf behind her. She crossed her hands on her chest and breathed another few minutes, staring up at the ceiling. Finally she said, "My mother's dying."

Linda was stunned. She'd met Dorothy McClellan just once, when Dot, as everyone called her, had come from Phoenix to visit for the July 4th weekend. Dot had been delightful. She had also been strong willed and opinionated, and Linda saw where Kirsten got her resolve. Dot McClellan was outgoing and affable, and a keen observer of people. Linda had been terrified Dot wouldn't like her, but all went well and when they drove Kirsten's mother to the airport in Philadelphia she hugged Linda and welcomed her to the family.

"Did you just say your mother was dying?"

"Well, not tomorrow. But eventually. Maybe a year, she says."

"But how?"

Kirsten kept her eyes on the ceiling and Linda realized she wanted to avoid being seen crying. Kirsten McClellan did not cry, at least not in view of anyone else.

"She had breast cancer three years ago," Kirsten said. "Double mastectomy, chemo, the works. They thought it was gone, but they were wrong."

Linda turned on her side. She took Kirsten's hand and held it. "I'm so sorry," she said. "We should go there. Now. Tomorrow."

"No," Kirsten said. "It's gone into her liver, her lymph nodes. It's bad this time, Linda, very bad. There's no escape. She refused to do chemo again, and I have to respect that. But she told me not to come, not yet. She wants me when she needs me—her words."

"When did you find this out?"

"Tuesday."

"And you didn't tell me?"

Kirsten rolled on her side to face Linda, and a tear rolled down onto the pillow. "Things take time with me," she said. "But I knew two things when I hung up that phone. I knew I would be there with my mother at the end of her life, and I knew I would spend mine with you."

Linda felt her own emotions rising up. Heartbreak and joy filled her. She had never known they could occupy the same space.

"If you want to live in a cave, Linda Sikorsky, then I'm moving to a cave with you. Sell it all and go live on the side of a mountain. Or the busiest city in the world. Or a dark country road where the crickets are so loud you just want to take a machine gun to them."

Kirsten laughed at that and Linda knew it was a small means of release. She had laughed many times at the stories her mother told her about her father Pete, all the while knowing each laugh hid a crack in her mother's heart.

"Will you marry me?" Kirsten said.

"You already asked me that. You put an engagement ring on my finger."

"I'm asking again. And it's not sometime, some place. It's soon. While my mother is alive to see it. Will you marry me?"

"Anytime, any place," said Linda, and she felt her own tears coming now.

The women held each other then, and after just another moment the damn broke. Kirsten McClellan, the real power in McClellan and Powers, began to sob.

# CHAPTER TWENTY-FOUR

Sonny felt better than he had in years, downright exhilarated. He had defied his mother for the first time. At twenty-nine, that made for a very long stretch of doing her bidding, letting her tell him where to go and what to do. But no more. She had told him to leave town, now. Take his girlfriend, get on his motorcycle and drive until they found some place off the grid, under the radar, far from where anyone could find them. He'd already lied to her about getting rid of the Mustang. It was a lie that let him know he could easily tell another. Why had he waited so long? Lying to Charlotte Gaines had come easy, and once he'd done it, he had no trouble doing it again. The nerve of her, demanding he run like some ground squirrel at the first sign of a hawk's shadow. He would not! He was Sonny Gaines. He was somebody, and he would prove it. Then he would leave and never look back.

Shirley stayed in the car a half mile down Route 651, off on the shoulder not far from where Abigail Creek had uttered her last scream. Fitting, Sonny thought, as he carried his gas can up the road. No one was up this time of night, nearly three o'clock in the morning. He knew the few lights he saw in houses were lights left on by the sleeping people inside them. Twice he heard a dog's bark and ignored it as he trudged slowly up the hill.

It was so dark here. The only light came from the stars and a moon two hundred thousand miles away. He was the moon, detached and watching his own actions. Like the moon, he did not care what came of the night. Maybe they would smell smoke and escape. Good for them. Or maybe they would awake to find themselves trapped by flames. Good for him. Either way it didn't matter to Sonny. He was here to finish a job, to make a point—and oh, would he make it.

He wasn't going into the house this time. There would be no apparition in a doorway to spook him. It had only been his imagination, but he was not taking chances tonight. He would stay outside, where ghosts did not venture. He saw the street sign for Lockatong Road in the moonlight. Almost there. He slowed his walk, pretending to be an Indian. He imagined himself a boy again, stalking his enemy in the woods. He always played the Indian, never the cowboy. Indians were so much cooler, and they killed without remorse. It was a matter of survival, and Sonny Gaines was a survivor. He'd outsmarted the most dangerous predator of all, his mother. He'd always been the winner back then, playing with his friends, and he would be the winner now.

He crept up the driveway, listening for the sound of his own footsteps and hearing nothing. Excellent! He let the gas can swing and adjust in his hand, the fuel inside it sloshing quietly back and forth. In another minute he was at the house, by the corner of the garage. It was the same garage he'd fled through the night before. He knew the garage was full of boxes and stored items, put there while Linda Sikorsky decided which of her aunt's belongings to part with and which to keep. It all made for excellent kindling and would spread the fire quickly.

He eased down on his haunches and removed the cap from the gas can. Carefully he tipped it up and watched as gasoline poured out onto the driveway and seeped under the garage door. He shifted foot to foot, sliding his way sideways along the garage door as he emptied the can, most of it pooling under the door and into the room of boxes.

Finally he was ready. He set the can down, the brief sound of its metal hitting blacktop the only noise he'd heard since leaving the car. He took the box of matches from his shirt pocket and paused. The time had come. He struck the match and was just about to toss it on the gas when he felt the gun barrel against the back of his head.

"Blow out the match," Linda said, "and I won't spread your skull on my driveway."

He'd heard nothing, not a twig snap, not a footstep, not the sound of her breathing. He stared at the burning match in his fingers. Another moment or two and it would singe him. He would drop it on the ground, where it would send the flames surging into the garage. And when he did, he knew she would kill him.

"I won't even count to three," said Linda. "You have exactly two seconds to blow out the match or die."

Sonny did not want to die, that much he could say. Not for his mother, not for revenge, not for anything. He blew out the match and tossed it to his side.

Linda eased the .45 away from his head but kept it aimed. "I saw you in town, talking to Charlotte Gaines. Now who are you? Did she hire you to kill us? The longer you take to answer, the more I'll know you're lying, so be quick."

"Ain't you gonna tell me to put my hands on the back of my head?" Sonny said, still crouching on the driveway.

"Nah," said Linda. "I need a clear shot."

Sonny Gaines felt the coldest chill he'd ever felt run from his toes up into his hair. He knew instantly this woman meant it, that she would shoot him dead on the spot and might enjoy doing it.

Linda stepped back just a little, allowing Sonny to turn slowly around in his crouch. He looked up at her and smiled. "I'm Sonny Gaines," he said. "The woman who sent me to kill you is my mother." It was a small stretch of the truth, but Sonny had no intention of taking the fall by himself.

"I'm sorry to hear that," Linda said. "But not all that surprised. Now let's go into the house. You can sit at the kitchen table while I call the police. Whatever plans you had for us or yourself have just ended."

Sonny did as he was told, slowly standing up and leading the way to the front door with Linda behind him, her father's gun ready to put an end to any plans Sonny Gaines would ever have again.

He thought he heard a car engine in the distance. It was impossible, he knew, to hear it this far away, but something told him Shirley was on her way. She had not wanted to do this. She had wanted to take Charlotte's advice—her command—and flee far and fast to the west somewhere. It had taken too long for Sonny to come back; or maybe she'd planned to leave him there all along. But somehow, through whatever means we know things, Sonny knew he was alone.

*But not for long, Mother*, he thought as he sat at Linda's kitchen table. *Not for long.*

# CHAPTER TWENTY-FIVE

Charlotte began to worry just after sunrise. At first she was glad Sonny had not called her from the road. The longer it took to hear from him, the further he and Shirley must have traveled—or so she thought. But it was now nearly eight o'clock in the morning and she had received no call, no email, no text. Something was wrong.

She had not slept more then a few hours. When this happened—and it happened more often than she would admit—she would lie next to Clarence on her side and stare at the wall. If she rolled on her back he might reach for her and know she was awake. The last thing she could appear to be was a woman worried about events she had set in motion. Poor, stupid, obstinate, vengeful Abigail. Had she settled for what she would get in the divorce, which was more than someone like Charlotte would ever see without a man like Clarence to provide it, she would be alive and none of this would be happening.

She made coffee in the kitchen and was taking a cup back to the bedroom for Clarence when she saw them arrive. Two cars: Linda and Kyle in one, the other a State Trooper's cruiser. She froze, a trembling cup of coffee in each hand. A moment later they all got out, the meddling ex-detective and her meddling friend, and Jackie Overly, looking like she'd been on duty all night. It hit her then: another death to report, another loss to be sorry for. Something had happened to someone, Justine perhaps … or Sonny. But that can't be, Charlotte thought. No one knew about Sonny, not even Clarence. Sonny had been her ace in the hole when she'd needed one, which had been several times throughout their lives. She told no one about Sonny, and Sonny told very few people about her. *They think you're my sister,* he said once. *It's embarrassing.* Whatever they were here for, Charlotte knew misfortune was about to visit CrossCreek Farm for the second time in three days.

"Clarence!" she called out. "Clarence, someone's here!"

She hurried and set the coffee cups down on the coffee table and walked to the door in her robe. Just as she was opening the door, Clarence Creek came out in his pajamas, running his hand through his hair. He'd not slept much the last few nights either, but for very different reasons. And unlike Charlotte, he had been expecting this visit.

"I'll get it," Clarence said, stepping in front of Charlotte and opening the door. "Good morning, Jackie. Detective ...?"

"Retired," Linda said. "Linda Sikorsky, and this is Kyle Callahan. Trooper Overly you know."

"Yes, of course, you were here Saturday. At the wake, too. Please come in." Clarence motioned them into the living room. He closed the door and joined them, with Charlotte close behind saying nothing.

"Is someone else dead?" Clarence said, getting to the point.

"Almost," Trooper Overly replied. She looked grim, as if this was the last visit she ever wanted to make.

"I don't understand."

"Someone tried to burn down my house last night," Linda said.

Charlotte felt her stomach drop and her heart freeze. She knew instantly why Sonny had not contacted her; she also knew he had defied her and likely cost them everything.

"If you'll excuse me," Charlotte said, turning toward the hallway.

"I'd rather you stay," said Trooper Overly. "At least in the house."

"Are you asking me?"

"Not really."

Knowing there was nowhere to run, Charlotte walked to a chair and sat down, bracing herself.

"You know," Linda said, "from the very beginning I thought Abigail wasn't killed for who she was, or that it was an accident. No one goes fleeing from a house in her nightgown and slippers, riding a bicycle down a dark road at night. I've thought all along she was killed for what she knew."

"That's ridiculous," Charlotte said. "What could Abigail possibly know that anyone would kill her for?"

"Let's start with the will," said Linda.

"My will?" Clarence said. "There's nothing in my will to kill anyone for. I was adding Justine back in, yes, Abi knew that. She didn't like it, but she knew it was my decision, my possessions to do with as I saw fit. We fought about it, but certainly not to the death."

"It's not your will I'm talking about." Linda reached into her purse and took out the copy of the deed that had given the land to Harlan Creek. "It's your grandfather's will. I think Abigail knew it was a forgery."

"You have a copy?" Clarence stared at the paper in Linda's hand as she unfolded it.

"No, not yet anyway. This is the deed to CrossCreek Farm, before it was called that. After Randall Davis died at the bottom of his own well. It has his signature on it." She held the paper out for Clarence to see, pointing at the signature. "I think it won't match the signature on the will. I also think you have a copy, and that somehow Abigail knew. She found it. Or maybe she had always known, but she kept the secret until there was no reason to. Until there was every reason to reveal it. She wanted it all—or at least she wanted you not to have it."

Clarence took the deed and looked at it a moment, then handed it back. "It's not a forgery, the signatures match. You can see for yourself, I have the original."

Linda felt her hopes vanishing. There was no question who had tried to set her house on fire; he was in the Hunterdon County Jail waiting to be processed. Sonny Gaines killed Abigail Creek, and Linda had believed she held the motive in her hand.

At the same time, Charlotte felt relief. There must be a way to play this, to let Sonny take the blame. She would have to admit she had a son, but she could explain it. She could say he was a bad seed, a very troubled child, and that was why she had never told Clarence about him. This might not turn out the way she feared.

"My grandfather was no fool," Clarence said. "He knew people would be suspicious. A forged will was a sure ticket to the gallows."

*Shut up*, Charlotte thought. *Don't say another word.*

"It wasn't the will Abigail found." Clarence decided then and there it was time to end this. It had cost the life of the woman he had two children with, the woman he had loved for all these years, despite the challenges of it. "It was a letter."

Charlotte felt herself go pale. She knew about the letter. She knew Abigail had found it. She was the one person in the room who knew everything, and the knowledge was about to destroy her.

"What letter is that, Clarence?" asked Trooper Overly.

"My grandfather's confession."

They waited silently a moment as Clarence gathered his thoughts.

"Harlan Creek wasn't a good man, not by any stretch. But he was a haunted man, with a guilty conscience. On his deathbed he wrote a letter confessing what he'd done to old Randall Davis, how he'd forced him at gunpoint to sign a will Harlan had written himself, then marched him outside. He killed him with a shovel to the head and threw his body down the well."

"I think you need a lawyer," Charlotte said, careful not to say "we."

Clarence dismissed her with a sharp wave of his hand. "No lawyer, no more secrets." He continued: "He'd rewritten the will a few days before killing Davis. The original left the land to Jacob Mullen. That's who this property was supposed to belong to when Randall Davis died."

"Clarence …" Charlotte said, trying to stop him.

"Shut up, Charlotte," he shot back. "Harlan gave the letter to my father. He never expected it to see the light of day—his conscience wasn't *that* guilty. He just didn't want to take his secret to the grave with him. Instead of destroying the letter, my father kept it. For posterity, I suppose. Or maybe he thought it might be useful someday … which it was. I kept it in my safe."

"And Abigail found it," Kyle said. "Or did she know all along?"

"No, she didn't know. It was in my personal safe. She had her own, for her jewelry and valuables. We were in the middle of the divorce negotiations and I'd gone into the safe for some papers. I can be as forgetful as the next person, and I left the safe open. The next thing I knew she had the letter and she said her demands had just changed."

"Why are you telling us this?" Linda asked.

"Because I've never told anyone else," Clarence said. "It's been a stone around my neck since I was a boy and first found out about the letter. All this has happened for property. I don't think it was worth it. It never was. I knew it was going to come out someday. I suppose that's why I kept it instead of burning it in the fireplace. I was ready to walk away from it all, to tell Abigail, here, take the letter, the house, the land, I don't want it anymore. And then she was killed."

Linda glanced at Charlotte, who was avoiding eye contact with all of them.

"Do you still have the letter?" Trooper Overly asked.

"No," he said. "Abigail kept it. I'm sure it's with her lawyer. He stood to make a tidy sum off our misery." He took a deep breath. "Now tell me, Jackie, why are you here?"

"For Charlotte," Jackie Overly said. She stood up then, addressing a trembling Charlotte directly. "Your son is in jail for murder and attempted murder. He's been talking since three o'clock this morning."

Clarence turned suddenly to Charlotte. "Son?" he said.

"I can explain," said Charlotte.

"You'll have a chance to do that," Jackie said. "Please get dressed, Charlotte. You're under arrest for the murder of Abigail Creek."

Clarence howled, "No!" and jumped up from the couch. Linda was afraid he was going to attack Charlotte and she slipped her hand to the gun in her purse. Instead, Clarence just stood in front of Charlotte, his face red as he shouted at her, "How could you do that! For a *vineyard*? Thirty acres of land that isn't even rightfully mine?"

Charlotte said nothing. Clarence might be foolish enough to speak without an attorney, but she was not. She could still pin this on Sonny. He was her son, after all, and finally she had reason to be glad of it. Sonny was the one who wanted his mother to gain from this marriage. Sonny was the one who felt threatened by Abigail's—and CrossCreek Farm's—secret. Sonny had done this on his own, and Charlotte had tried to stop him. She was about to go to the police herself, then it had all come to this. She was spinning her story in her head as she headed to the bedroom to get dressed. Trooper Jackie Overly followed her. A woman like this might try to flee, and Jackie would not take her eyes off her.

Clarence eased back onto the couch. "Charlotte has a son?" he said weakly.

"More like a viper," Linda said. "He told us he came here to scare Abigail, that he had no intention of killing her."

"Most likely a lie," Kyle added.

"It didn't go as planned. Abigail ran out of the house and down the road on the bicycle. He chased after her in his car … and we know what happened then."

"But how could she not tell me all this time she had a son?"

Linda looked at him. "How could you not tell Sly Mullen all this time that CrossCreek Farm belonged to him? How could you not tell his father?"

"I had nothing to do with what happened," Clarence said, knowing it was not true. To keep someone else's secret is to be complicit in it.

"To the contrary, Mr. Creek," Linda said. "I think you had everything to do with it."

They sat in silence then. Ten long minutes later Charlotte came back into the room. She had not put on her makeup. She had not even showered. She had simply dressed in jeans and a blouse, gotten her purse and hung it on her arm. She was followed by Jackie Overly. The time had come.

"Tell me you weren't part of this," Clarence said.

Charlotte stared at him. "Everyone was part of it. Your leeching son, your vengeful wife, your father, your grandfather. No one in this family was not part of it. Except maybe Justine. She's the only one I ever really liked." She turned to Jackie Overly and said, "Let's go."

Linda and Kyle had no reason or desire to stay. They got up and walked out of the house behind Charlotte and Jackie. Clarence followed, standing in the doorway as they walked to their cars.

"You're still coming to the funeral, I hope," he called out.

Linda turned back. She thought a moment, then said, "Yes, Mr. Creek. We'll be there. We found her on the road. It's only proper we be there to bury her."

They got in their cars, with Charlotte in the back of the cruiser staring straight ahead. She would have nothing more to say until the best attorney money could buy was at her side. A moment later they were gone.

Clarence stood in the doorway looking out at the empty driveway. He knew Caroline and Rusty would be along soon, wondering what all the activity had been about. He had a long story to tell them before letting them know it was time to leave CrossCreek Farm. All of them.

# CHAPTER TWENTY-SIX

It was the second funeral Linda had been two in three months. She had buried her aunt Celeste in Doylestown, next to her husband. It was not a family plot; there was no third space for their son, Jeffrey Dickerson. That service had been much smaller. Celeste was beloved and popular, but had not wanted a show and only immediate family members were invited, including Linda's mother Estelle. Abigail's funeral, on the other hand, was a testament to what she must have felt was her place in the community. Nearly everyone at the wake had shown up, despite the steady drizzle that had started overnight.

Clarence, Caroline and Rusty were seated in the front row, almost within arm's reach of the casket that rested on a hydraulic platform. Once everyone was gone, the gravediggers would ease the casket down into the earth and fill it in. Abigail's final goodbye.

Linda, Kyle, Danny and Kirsten were among the last to arrive. There were no seats left, so they stood quietly in the back and listened as a local pastor gave a scripted eulogy. Abigail was beloved. Abigail was a pillar of the community. Abigail was being entrusted to the Lord. Each of the Creeks, with the exception of the absent Justine, walked the few feet from their chairs and tossed a white rose onto the casket.

"Do you think she knows we caught her killer?" Kyle asked. He hated funerals and planned to have none for himself. He and Danny had agreed that each would be cremated. Kyle didn't even want a memorial, but he'd left that up to Danny, knowing such things are for the living.

"I doubt she knows anything," Linda said. "Not to be disrespectful."

"It would be nice, though."

Nice to know Charlotte was already out on bail, and out of CrossCreek Farm. Clarence had not even allowed her back in to get her belongings. She had proclaimed her innocence and insisted Sonny had acted on his own, but Clarence did not believe her. And even if he did—even though he wanted to—he would never let her back into his life. He felt humiliated at having been such a fool. An old man falling in love, he told himself, when love had been a disguise for greed. Had he ever known someone as greedy as Charlotte Gaines? The only one who came close was being buried, and for Abigail it had been more anger than greed. She didn't want CrossCreek Farm. She wanted Clarence, and if she couldn't have him, then she would take the very thing she believed defined him. But she had been wrong.

After the service, as Linda and the others made their way back across the lawn, Clarence called out, "Ms. Sikorsky! Ms. Sikorsky!" She stopped and waited for him as the other mourners all headed to the line of cars parked along the cemetery drive.

"Go on to the car," Linda told them. Kyle, Danny and Kirsten headed on, leaving Linda to stand quietly while Clarence hurried up to her.

"I wanted to tell you I'm sorry," Clarence said.

"There's nothing to be sorry for," Linda replied. "Not to me, any-way." She glanced behind him at the gravesite.

"I don't agree," he said. "You've been part of this from the begin-ning, ever since you drove down that road Friday night and found Abigail. And Sonny Gaines …"

"He's in jail, Mr. Creek."

"Clarence."

"He's in jail and he's probably going to stay there the rest of his life, with a transfer to prison, of course. The judge denied bail."

"I know that wasn't the case with Charlotte. She insists she wasn't involved."

"She's lying."

"I believe you. But she got bail and paid it. She also has a very good lawyer, I'm told. I don't know how she's paying for these things."

Linda looked at him. "I'd check my account balances if I were you."

"You really think she's that evil?"

"I don't know what her reasons are for being that way, but yes."

"And you don't think there's any chance she wasn't behind all this?"

Linda let silence be her response. "What are you going to do now, Clarence? With the farm, I mean? Are you going to tell Sly Mullen –"

"He already knows. The property is his. It always has been. And this won't be some long drawn out legal situation. We'll be out by the end of the month."

Linda was startled. Things were moving very fast for the Creeks. "Where will you all go?"

"Where Caroline and Rusty go is not my concern. That's one wish of Abigail's that's finally come true. As for me, I don't know yet. Justine has always wanted a small house. I think I may find one big enough for two."

"She didn't come," Linda said.

"Do you blame her?"

Linda did not. Staying away from the Creeks had kept Justine untainted by the events of the last three days. "I'm glad I was here, but it's time to go now," she said. "I'm sorry for your loss, really. I've said that a hundred times in my profession, but I mean it."

She started to leave. He gently put his hand on her arm and stopped her.

"Abigail was a good woman," he said. "I want you to know that. She was a good woman, and a wronged one. I can't say I blame her for hating me."

Linda patted his hand. "I don't think she hated you at all. I think she loved you very much."

With that Linda let his hand slip away, turned and walked toward her car.

Clarence Creek watched her go. Just as she was nearly out of earshot, he said, "Maybe something good will grow there now."

Linda was reminded of what Clara had said at the Inn, her grandmother's warning. *Whatever grows there, grows in the shadows.* Sunlight had made its way in all these years later. Maybe Clarence Creek was right. Maybe something good would grow there with them gone.

The drizzle had stopped. Linda made her way in the wet grass up to the drive. She remained silent as she got in the car, fastened her seatbelt, and drove them away from a cemetery she hoped to never see again.

# CHAPTER TWENTY-SEVEN

Kyle sat on the back porch with Danny and Linda. Yesterday's rain had moved on and the early morning sun bathed the back yard in bright, warm light. It was the best weather day they'd had there. It was also their last. Kyle wondered why it sometimes worked that way. Their vacation had been spent solving a murder instead of sightseeing, shopping and eating in the many restaurants the area had to offer.

"It seems to be a pattern," Kyle said, sipping the last cup of coffee he would have on this trip to Detective Linda's house.

"Sitting on the porch having coffee?" said Linda. The morning's perfection wasn't lost on her. She only wished Kirsten was with them, but she knew three nights in a row was a record and she was grateful for that. She would take her turn tonight and head to New Hope, staying at Kirsten's condo. They were spending nearly every night together now, and Linda wondered why she had been so worried. Her mother said expectations were disappointments waiting to happen, something she'd always thought wise until she had expectations of her own. She and Kirsten would be heading to Phoenix in a week, the first of many trips Linda knew they would be taking during the time Dot McClellan had left on this earth.

"He means getting caught up in other people's deaths," Danny said. "You, Kyle, murder. It's become an equation."

"It's not like we go looking for it," Kyle said.

"I'm not so sure about that."

A car drove past on the front road, backfiring as it headed toward the highway.

"There's a sound you don't hear much around here," Linda said. She was getting used to life in the country. She'd realized it had its own distinct sights and sounds, and each was slowly becoming part of her.

"I wish we could have met your aunt," said Kyle. "She sounds like a remarkable woman."

"She was. And she was a lot like my father. I know it's an odd thing to say, since he died when I was only eight years old, but I remember things about him. His presence, his laugh. Aunt Celeste had the same laugh. Do you think laughs are genetic?"

"Just about everything is," Danny said. "The people we love, the things we love doing, so much of it seems hardwired into us."

Kyle looked at Linda: she was becoming hardwired into him. He hadn't had a close female friend in a long time, other than his boss Imogene. Was this life's way of giving him a replacement, to soften the blow of Imogene's departure? He was sure it was coming.

"What do you think's going to happen to the Creeks?" Kyle asked.

"I have no idea," Linda replied. "And I'm not so sure I want to know. The land will go to Sly Mullen, Sonny Gaines will spend most of his life in prison, if not all of it. Charlotte—who knows? She seems very resourceful, in the worst way."

Danny looked at his watch. It was nearly nine o'clock and he had an appointment that afternoon with Chloe at the restaurant. He sensed things changing, too. Margaret would likely be leaving within the year, heading to Florida to spend her last few years with her sister. The cats were getting older; they were all getting older.

"May twelfth," Danny said suddenly.

"What about it?" said Kyle.

"That's our wedding day. May twelfth, next spring. Save the date, Detective, there can't be a wedding without you."

Kyle was surprised. He knew they would marry, but he hadn't expected it to be so definite, so soon. May was only six months away. There was a lot of planning to do and they would have to start soon. Still, his heart leapt at the thought of finally marrying Danny. It felt like the last bit of this particular journey, a kind of finish line beyond which they would walk the road together to its end, the slower the better.

"What's so special about May twelfth?" he asked.

Danny stared at him. "Are you serious?"

It hit Kyle then: May twelfth was the night he met Danny at the Katherine Pride Gallery. He'd always considered their anniversary to be their first date two weeks later.

"I'm just joking."

"No, you're not," Danny said. "You didn't remember, and it's okay. Now you'll never forget."

Linda said, "The date is set. And pretty soon you'll have one to save, too. Kirsten and I are getting married."

"We knew that," said Kyle.

"Well, I wish you'd told me! I wasn't so sure. But Kirsten's mother in Phoenix is very sick." She hesitated, not sure Kirsten wanted her sharing this information. "I'll leave it to Kirsten to tell you more, but I imagine we'll be marrying in the next year."

Kyle was struck by how quickly things changed. Just two years ago he and Danny couldn't marry in their own state. Now he only had to wait six more months. He would gladly go to City Hall tomorrow, but he knew Danny wanted a wedding—and his mother wanted a wedding, and Danny's parents wanted a wedding. Everyone wanted a wedding, so he and Danny would give them one.

"It's time to get going," Danny said. He stood up from the table and took his and Kyle's cups.

"I was hoping you'd stay another week," Linda said, pushing her chair out.

"We'll be back," said Kyle. "We don't have to go to Pride Lodge anymore. We've got a place in the country to stay for free! And speaking of visits ..."

"Yes?"

"I think you and Kirsten should come to Pride Weekend in June."

Linda had never been to a Pride Parade. She'd never even been back to New York City until last spring for Kyle's exhibit. Thirty-five years in the desert. Thirty-five years in the closet. That was all past her now, and she liked the idea of standing on a Manhattan sidewalk with a million other people watching one of the city's most festive parades.

"It's a date," Linda said.

"A date, and a parade! What can go wrong?"

Danny frowned. What can go wrong when Kyle and Detective Linda got together? Plenty. He took the cups and headed into the house, with Kyle and Linda close behind. It was time to go home now, back to the cats Smelly and Leonard, back to Margaret and Imogene. Back to the life they'd shared for years that passed more rapidly with each one. *Time is on no one's side*, Danny thought, then shook it off. *Time is not the enemy. Time takes no sides. It only is, and what you do with it determines the fullness of your life.* He turned to Kyle just as they entered the house. "I love you," he said.

The door closed behind them, the sun continued climbing the sky. Another day was passing and waiting for them to come along.

# UP NEXT: THE PRIDE TRILOGY CONCLUDES

First there was *Murder at Pride Lodge*. A mysterious visitor travels halfway across the country to an idyllic gay resort seeking vengeance after thirty years. Detective Linda Sikorsky investigates the death at Pride Lodge and becomes life-long friends with Kyle Callahan and his partner Danny Durban, there for a weekend of Halloween festivities. The fun ends abruptly with the death of Teddy the handyman, his broken body discovered at the bottom of an empty pool, and they find themselves working feverishly to solve a murder—if a murder was even committed!

Next came *Pride and Perilous*. Amateur photographer Kyle is having his first photography exhibit at the Katherine Pride Gallery in Manhattan's Meatpacking District. An acquaintance is brutally murdered on a dark, rainy Brooklyn street, and Kyle quickly realizes someone wants this gallery closed forever. Joined once again by his friend Detective Linda, they must find out who is killing people connected to the gallery and why, before another body falls.

And now … *Death by Pride*, the final book in the Pride Trilogy. A body is found in Manhattan's East River on a late June night. Reading about it the next day, Kyle discovers to his horror that the Pride Killer has returned to New York City. It's been three years and the elusive serial killer was thought to have vanished, but Pride Weekend approaches and no one doubts he has come back more deadly than ever. Detective Linda returns to the city for her first Pride Weekend, looking forward to a spectacular parade. Instead she finds herself once more in the hunt with Kyle, in the most dangerous pursuit of their lives.

# DEATH BY PRIDE
# CHAPTER ONE
## NEW MOON

Killing wasn't as much fun as it used to be. He expected to be a bit rusty after three years, but he had never anticipated this ... *dullness*, this sense that, in the words of bluesman B.B. King, the thrill was gone. Maybe he had just been away from it too long; maybe he needed to get up to speed. The man whose body he deposited into the East River just before midnight was, after all, only the first in his current series. There would be two more before the week was out, and maybe the old rush would return with the next one. He had to trust it would, to believe as a child believes that Santa Claus is real and will come shimmying down the chimney every Christmas Eve. Or how Dorothy believed, clicking her slippers in that dreadful movie. That might be a more appropriate comparison, given the occasion. Click, click, click ... and he was home.

He did not come all the way back to New York to resume his annual ritual for something as lackluster as this first kill. Had it been the young man himself who stirred so little response in him? What was his name, Victor? Victor Somebody. Dense and inattentive; he had been too easy. Yes, that must be it. Like a cat who had no trouble capturing a wingless bird, he had not had fun with this one. He would have to analyze the experience, figure out why it had not been as satisfying as it was before, and what he might need to do to reignite his excitement. Did he need to be more brutal? Did he need to introduce tools into the game? He would think hard on it. A decision had to be made quickly; he'd already placed an online ad looking for the next one and the emails were flooding into his special account, the one no one would ever trace no matter how hard they tried. A phantom as elusive as he was deserved a phantom email.

Deidrich Kristof Keller III—D to everyone who knew him well (a thought that made him chuckle, since the only ones who truly knew him died with the knowledge) had only been back in his townhouse since March. His tenants, the ones he rented to when he left for Berlin to take care of his mother, had a lease through February and D had waited patiently for them to leave. A lovely young couple with two small children. He'd never met Susan and Oliver Storch—the rental had been arranged through an agent—but they had taken very good care of the place, he would give them that. And you would never know they had children; no stray toys were left behind, no evidence, really, that anyone had been there at all for the past three years. His kind of people, he thought, and smiled.

He was so glad to be back. He'd hated Berlin, all of Germany for that matter, though he saw very little of it and had no desire to see more. For D being German was as meaningless as someone being Scottish who had never been to Scotland, spoke with no brogue, and was only tied to the land by name and ancestry. His parents were from Germany, but they had moved to Anaheim, California, before D was born. His mother, Marta, returned to Berlin a broken, bitter woman, but that was not his fault. She was a coward. *Cowardess?* he wondered, making a cup of tea at his kitchen counter. It was an island counter, surrounded by a stove and refrigerator large enough to impress and too large to be practical— there was almost nothing in the refrigerator, and he rarely cooked. The entire townhouse was furnished for show—the furniture, the artwork, the paintings and photographs of nonexistent family members and fore-bears. It had been carefully put together to deceive. Anyone who came into his home would think he was just another wealthy man in New York City with a long lineage, should one wonder where he came from. Men with paintings of their grandfathers above a fireplace surely belonged in Manhattan's upper reaches and had unquestionable pedigree. That was the point, to be unquestioned. By the time anyone got around to questioning him, to wondering about his authenticity, it was too late. He answered their questions with a belt around their necks. *You're right, good man, I'm not who I appear to be. Please keep that to yourself.* And they did.

He was tired now. He'd worked out how to get the bodies out of his house unnoticed some years ago, but he was getting older, forty-two this coming September. It wasn't as easy as it used to be. And this one had been fatter than he'd remembered when he chose him.

*Note to self: never, ever, pick a customer from the store again. Stay online, stay hidden behind a dozen re-routers, change names each time, do not take this risk again.*

Victor Somebody. He would look at the man's driver's license in the morning. It was his souvenir—his thirteenth. Lucky thirteen. The rest of the wallet stayed with the body. He wasn't interested in making identification difficult. It didn't matter if the police knew who had been killed, only that they would never find the man who did the killing.

It had been dark when he parked by the river. The new moon had worked to his favor, a first. No one had been around; he made sure no one saw a man with a heavy, strangely shaped object wrapped in black plastic trudging his way to the river's edge. Then a simple heave and splash, and he was on his way home.

Bedtime at last. But before then, for a few minutes anyway, he wanted to go through those emails. He'd requested photos, knowing many of them would be old and meant to trick him, and that was okay. He was less interested in finding a man who looked exactly like his picture than he was in finding a man who made him want to kill. It was like falling in love with an image: he never knew which one it would be, but knew it when it happened. *This one. Oh yes. This one will be here soon.*

He turned off the kitchen light, took his tea cup with the little chain from the tea ball hanging over the side, and headed to his large master bedroom on the second floor. His laptop was open and waiting for him. He would sift through a dozen or so email responses and see if any of them struck his fancy. But first, the pictures of Victor. Victor Somebody. He would enjoy those before sleeping. He always took pictures.

# ABOUT THE AUTHOR

Writing is the one thing I have done consistently all my life, whether it was being expressed in short fiction, long fiction, poetry, prose, plays, or children's television scripts. It is the one thing I have always felt compelled to do. I've had dozens of short stories and articles published, six plays produced, and capped off my time in children's television with an Emmy in 2001 for Outstanding Children's Program in the Chicago/Milwaukee market.

'Death in the Headlights' is the third book in the Kyle Callahan Mysteries series. It was a needed departure from the Pride Trilogy, which will conclude with the next book, 'Death by Pride.'

Thanks to anyone and everyone who has set a spell with Kyle and the gang. I hope you'll take another ride on the mystery train, meet a new traveler or two, and keep me getting up before the sun to bring you more!

As for my personal life, I live in New York City with my husband Frank Murray and our three cats. We have a house in the rural New Jersey countryside where we plan to move permanently someday ... maybe.

CPSIA information can be obtained
at www.ICGtesting.com
Printed in the USA
BVOW06s1922011117
499283BV00009B/241/P